Man of Mystery

L. MOONE

CONTENTS

PART ONE

CHAPTER ONE

What a day. I sigh and rest my forehead against the steering wheel. After getting called in for my semi-annual appraisal and having all my achievements from the past six months swept under the rug because Karen took credit for them, I can't imagine how today could get any worse.

Of course, traffic can always worsen any day. It's warm, too warm to be driving a twenty-year-old rust-bucket without air conditioning. And opening the window does nothing except let in more hot air and fumes from the thousands of cars surrounding me in what has got to be a record for west London. The traffic is spectacularly horrible for a Thursday.

Can't I catch a fucking break?

I pick up my mobile and after scanning the surrounding vehicles, I figure it's safe enough to make a call. No coppers around at the moment. The last thing I need is another ticket.

"Hey, Maggie?" I say, greeting the groggy voice on the other end of the line.

"Yeah, Tess, what's up?"

"Nothing. Same old, life's a bitch. Shall we go out tonight? I could use the distraction." The car ahead of me moves but I decide it's not worth the effort to put mine in first gear, just to creep ahead four feet.

"Sounds great, but I have a date, and then straight to work. Another day perhaps?" Maggie yawns on the other end. Typical, ever since she's started working the midnight shift at the airport, her routine has been all over the place.

"A date, huh? I'm jealous. Who's the lucky guy?" I ask, even though I already suspect it's that guy she works with, Alec, whom she's been going on about nonstop lately.

"I finally decided enough is enough and asked out Alec. You know nowadays you can't sit back and wait for men to make the first move. That's all in the past. The dating scene is all about equal opportunities."

"Mhm, if you say so. I guess I'm a bit old-fashioned that way." *Which is probably why I haven't had a date in months.*

"Say, you wanna talk about what's going on? I have a little while before I need to start getting ready."

"Thanks. Well, as I said. Same old." I sigh, and squeeze the bridge of my nose to get rid of the beginnings of a tension headache.

"Your boss, Frank-something still bothering you?"

"No, I mean yes. Sort of. I had my appraisal today. Can you believe it? Of all my suggestions which were actually implemented these past six months, none of that was mentioned. That tart I told you about,

Karen, presented everything like it was her idea, after making me do the groundwork. And now it looks like I've been doing fuck all and I'm not pulling my weight," I rant.

"I see. Same old indeed. What can you do? People like her will do anything to get ahead, even if it means trampling those in her way. Keep calm, bide your time and return the favour or find another job. No other option."

"Another job where? I ought to be grateful I have one at all with the way things have been going." I take a deep breath and grip the steering wheel tighter until my knuckles turn white. I wonder if things ever get easier.

"True. If you ever change your mind on shift work, I could ask around at work?"

"Thanks, Maggie. That's very sweet. I'll let you know." I'm getting desperate, but I'm not ready to work nights. Yet.

"Sure thing, Tess. OK, I'd better have a shower and all. I want to look my best for tonight."

"Break a leg. And if he turns out to be a prat, I'll break both of his."

"Cheers. I'll let you know how it goes."

I put down the phone again, feeling slightly better after venting to Maggie. What are friends for, eh? The space in front of my car has opened up even further and I finally do pull ahead.

Metal boxes in all shapes and sizes as far as the eye can see. Perhaps there's an accident up ahead. It's going to take at least an hour to get to the motorway from here in this mess. That means I won't make it home until God knows when.

Urgh. I rest my head back on the steering, wondering if anyone would notice if I had a short nap behind the wheel.

The click of my rear door followed by a gust of air causes a cold shiver to creep down my spine. *Someone's behind me!*

"What the hell?" I instinctively snatch up my handbag and phone from the passenger seat while turning around as best I can to face the intruder.

"Shh…" The man cowering half on the back seat makes a calming motion with his hand, but doesn't look directly at me. My heart is hammering in my throat, threatening to make me freeze up, but I react almost on autopilot anyway.

"Get out! Get the hell out of my car!" I shout, while rummaging furiously in my purse. "I have pepper spray." My fingers grasp a small deodorant bottle. "And I'm not afraid to use it!"

"Be careful with that, if you blind yourself we're both done for." His gentle and calm tone surprises me. If he's trying to mug me, he's got a strange technique.

"I… what do you mean, we're both done for?"

I'm still pointing the deodorant bottle in his general direction, but am suddenly not so sure I want to spray him with it.

"I need you to drive. I swear I have a good reason to get into your car. Also, you've got that the wrong way around."

My fingers shake even more intensely as he reaches out for the can, and twists the nozzle in his direction.

"There."

"Shit. I'm sorry. Thanks. I mean…" *Why the hell am I apologising to this criminal?* Still, I feel like a total idiot for threatening to spray him with what is essentially perfume. I suppose it would hurt if it ends up in his eye, but it's not quite mace, is it? I lower my hand and take a proper look at him.

The stranger is still sort of hiding half in the foot well and half on the seat, skittishly looking out the window, while sneaking glances in my direction. He doesn't look like a mugger. But then, I've never been mugged, how would I know what a mugger looks like?

Still, his suit and shirt make him look more like a businessman than a criminal. Or a waiter perhaps.

"Good thing you're no longer intent on making me smell like… Lush Lavender, is it? Yeah. Not really my style," he says with a subtle smile on his face.

A joke, really? Now?

"There's no accounting for taste," I respond, while keeping my gaze fixed on his eyes. Green, bright, focused. "Now, if you don't mind explaining yourself."

"Of course. What would you say if I told you that there are some very bad people heading to Heathrow right now with a cargo that could destroy the world as we know it?" he says.

"I would ask if you've been drinking." I continue to stare at him, but he's unfazed by my reaction and smiles again. How is he so calm? This whole thing has got to be a joke.

"Fair enough."

"And anyway if it's Heathrow you're headed for, you'd probably be faster walking at this rate." I point forward at the traffic to emphasise my point.

"I'm sure you could find a faster route if you put your mind to it," he responds while pointing at the left turn just ahead.

If I hurry, I can get out of the queue heading to the motorway and make my way through the housing estate until I get to the A30, and then... *Wait, why should I help this clown?*

"Why should I take you to Heathrow? You could be a lunatic. Or you could in fact be the person taking said terrible cargo to Heathrow yourself. I don't know you!"

He looks up at me again, his eyes boring into me.

There's something about him that makes me want to trust him, but at the same time the sensible voice in my head insists I'm being an idiot.

"Look, I would show you my badge, but I don't have it on me. This whole mess unfolded while I was off duty, my unit's been compromised and time is of the essence." His face is dead serious now, and I hesitate to argue with him any further, but still, it's all so surreal I can't just accept it.

"What unit? You can't expect to just invade a stranger's car and commandeer it to take you to the airport. I've had a trying day and am just trying to get home, OK? I can't get involved in some crazy plot…"

"Shh… look straight ahead. We're probably being watched and I don't want you drawing attention to me in the back here. If I had another option I wouldn't have gotten in, but I didn't."

I give him one more glance and then look forward while scanning the surroundings from the corner of my eye. I don't see anyone watching… There's a guy waiting at the bus stop, but seems to be fiddling with his phone.

"There's nobody there, just the guy at the bus stop."

"Is he wearing black commando boots?"

"I don't know, I can't see properly from here. Yes. Maybe." I squint to get a better look, even though he's still focused on his phone and as such totally harmless.

"There you go. If he's wearing boots, he's one of them." The stranger shuffles around behind me, bumping into my seat.

Although I do my best to stay straight, I can't see what he's doing from the mirror and my nerves get the better of me so I turn around real quick anyway. "What the fuck? Is that a real gun?" I turn fully now, shocked at what I'm seeing. "Now what, you're going to threaten me so I take you to the airport? Hell no, I can't deal with this today, I just can't."

"Shush!" he hisses. "Yes it's a gun. No, I'm not threatening you, it's for protection in case the guy spots us. Now if you don't mind taking that turn and getting the hell out of here, I'd really appreciate it."

"I… He's just on the phone… I think you're overreacting." I look up again, but the man in the boots is no longer waiting at the bus stop. Panic washes over me at once. *Shit, what if this guy is right?* I slam the car into first, release the clutch way too quickly, making the car jump and squeal ahead and take the left turn into the

residential area. I think I can see that man running after the car in my rear view mirror, but perhaps that's just my mind playing tricks on me.

CHAPTER TWO

———— ◆ ————

"Happy now?" I complain, while steering the car through the tight zig-zagging roads, heading for the other side of the housing estate. "Heathrow it is. What terminal?"

"Uhh..."

"Don't tell me you don't know? Do you have any idea how huge Heathrow is?" I exclaim.

"Give me a moment."

I turn to find the stranger looking at a phone-type device, just fatter, like a handheld satnav thing for hikers. My ex had something similar he took on treks.

"Four. Terminal 4."

"Great." I put my foot down as I join the A30, all the while keeping an eye on my speedo which is close to touching fifty miles an hour. "How much time do we have?"

"Not much. Do your best," he says, while giving me a quick pat on the shoulder. I don't know whether it's the adrenaline coursing through my body, or the fact that actually he's pretty hot for a crazy person, but his touch has an instant effect on me. I must be losing my mind to let this guy affect me at all.

"Fine. But if I get a ticket, I'm telling them you drove. I've got six points on my licence already and the insurance company will have me over a barrel if I get more," I ramble, my voice trembling slightly.

He lets out a chuckle and pats my shoulder again. "Deal. Now go."

He was right, once I put my mind to it, our progress towards Heathrow has greatly improved. I know these roads like the back of my hand, even if I still compulsively slow down at the speed camera leading up to the Terminal 4 ramp. I'm in this now, whether I want to be or not, but still I'm not willing to blatantly speed through a speed trap.

"We'll reach it soon, then what? Do I park up, or what?"

I check my mirror, seeing that he's sitting upright now, staring out the rear window.

"Actually, let me out just there." He points at the mini roundabout ahead of us. "The cargo is headed for flight SV118 departing for Riyadh at eighteen-fifty. I'm going to try and intercept it. Pull over."

I slam on the brakes and turn to face him properly. His face is tense yet determined, as he gazes ahead through the metal fence surrounding the cargo area ahead of us.

"What's your name?" he asks, leaning forward and making eye contact again.

"Tess…" I mumble, severely distracted by the green depths in front of me again. Shit, why do I have a knack for attracting crazies? He's handsome though, the strong jawline, dark brown hair and symmetrical features are practically perfect. He could be a model, or an actor. Could all this just be an act?

"Tess. I know I'm asking a lot of you, but your country needs you." He pauses, his eyes lingering on my lips for a moment. "We can't let the plane leave. Give me your phone."

I hand it to him without protest. How is it that his eyes can hypnotise me like this? Shit, I must be desperate to be so easily distracted by a handsome guy in a suit. Once all this is over, I'm going to get Maggie to set me up with someone. She's been offering for weeks.

The stranger types a number into my phone and hits 'dial', then gives it back to me.

"I need you to go into the terminal and keep an eye on the departures board. If I'm successful, it will show up as delayed. If not, then you'll see its status change to 'boarding' at around eighteen-twenty. If that's the case, I need you to call in a bomb threat to shut down the terminal. Do you understand?" He reaches out for my cheek, caressing it with the back of his finger and causing even more upheaval inside my stomach. This has got to be a dream, even if it feels totally real.

I nod though. If the plane boards, I call the airport with a bomb threat. Sounds easy.

"Wait, why don't you just report a bomb threat

anyway? Why go through all this nonsense?" I ask.

He smiles briefly, pulling his hand back. "If I go in by myself, I may be able to detain some of the people involved. They may have intel. If I call it in now and the airport gets shut down, they'll run and we may never know who was behind it."

That makes sense, I guess.

I nod. "Fine. I'll go in."

"I'll be in touch if it went well."

"And if not?" I ask.

"Chances are, then I'll be dead."

He pushes his gun back into a holster on his calf, then opens the door and jumps out of the car, runs towards the fence and swiftly climbs over the top of it as if it's nothing. He must really keep fit to be able to do that. I wouldn't even make it halfway up, I'm sure.

I have to force myself to stop looking at him sprinting over the concrete beyond the fence, towards the hangars in the distance, and re-join the road. Following the instructions to the terminal parking, I leave my car in the first space I can find.

Once inside, I'm overwhelmed by the amount of people, shops, bright lights, boards. The earlier events in my car seem weirder and more unlikely than ever. After taking a moment to find my bearings, I make my way towards the first departures board I can find. It's only seventeen-twenty, plenty of time for him—whatever his name is—to stop the flight, right?

I was quick to agree to call in about a bomb when he pressed me in the car, but now that I'm on my own again, I'm not so sure. If I use my phone, they'll trace it and know it was me, perhaps I should use a pay phone. But then I'm sure they'd have me on CCTV, so if I don't want to get in trouble afterwards, I'll need a disguise.

I'm still undecided regarding what to do, when my phone buzzes once. A message. Just as I'm about to open it, do I see a familiar figure near the terminal entrance. The guy from the bus stop.

Damn, the stranger was right. All the buses stopping at the spot where this guy waited are going towards the city, not the airport, yet here he is. He *was* after us. Luckily the bad guy hasn't spotted me yet, so I casually slip away behind a pillar and quickly check the message.

Maggie: *'Alec cancelled on me, he's got flu. Still want to meet up?'*

I let out a sigh of relief. I don't know what I was expecting this message to be. A quick peek around the pillar reveals the bad guy has started wandering off towards the security check. It should be safe to respond:

'Later. Stuck in traffic.'

Moments later, it buzzes again, that'll be Maggie acknowledging my delay. I don't bother checking it, instead I look for a seat in one of the coffee shops overlooking yet another departures board. From here I'll be able to keep an eye on things without standing out. I order a latte and grab a newspaper from the stand in the corner. After settling down with everything, I feel like I'm on a proper stakeout. As if I'm looking out for bad guys rather than just a stupid board with flight information.

Minute after minute passes, and nothing on the board changes. It's too early. My latte is nearly finished and I've pretended to read the same paper twice already. At this rate, my efforts to blend in are going to make me look more suspicious.

Then, off towards the far side of the terminal hall, I see yet another familiar face entering through the large glass sliding doors. Alec. Although I've never met the guy, I'm certain it's him. Maggie had shown me a few pictures last time we met.

That's weird, he cancelled on their date and now he's here hours before his shift? Seeing as I've got nothing but time right now, and sitting here is just going to look weird, I decide to follow Alec. He won't recognise me so it should be quite safe. I owe it to Maggie to figure out why he would lie to her.

After folding up the newspaper, I grab my handbag and wander off somewhat aimlessly, though roughly in Alec's direction. What do people do here when they have to wait? The bright lights of some high end luggage shop catch my eye, so that's where I go to pretend to look at their display, though actually I'm observing Alec's reflection in the shop window.

He's checking his phone, and looking around the terminal as though he's looking for someone. Then he walks off towards the check-in desks. I follow, taking care to leave sufficient space and other travellers between us to avoid suspicion.

Just when I feel I'm tailing him like a pro, Alec opens a door labelled 'No Entry for Unauthorised Persons' and I've lost him. *Shit*. If I follow, I'll definitely get caught. And what am I doing anyway? Spying on Maggie's not-quite-boyfriend because he blew off their date saying he was sick? How lame.

I turn to head back to the coffee shop. If I order another coffee and perhaps a chocolate chip muffin, that'll buy me some time to babysit the departures board. I might even buy a magazine from WH Smith next door so I don't get totally bored.

Just as I start walking, I see the same door open again from the corner of my eye. Alec is back out and heading straight for the row of check-in desks nearest to us with his staff ID bouncing furiously off his chest with every brisk step he takes. Weird. Maggie told me he works with her in security…

I turn again and pause, while pretending to check the time on my watch. In my peripheral vision I can make out Alec heading directly to the Business Class desk. He talks to the girl currently manning the computer, shows her his ID and gestures for a bit until she gets up, clearly distraught, freeing up her seat for him.

As the girl rushes back towards the staff area Alec had just come from, he settles in and calls up the next two persons waiting in the queue ahead of him. As much as I am fond of Maggie, I'm not going to spy on this guy working his shift for her.

The moment I turn back towards the coffee shop, I see a familiar face about thirty feet away, the scary guy from the bus stop heading right towards me. Damn, he sees me! My throat tightens as I try to think of what to do. If I run, that would be weird, plus he would most definitely catch me. But what is he going to do in a public place with so many witnesses? Surely he can't do anything, can he?

And what have I done? Nothing. I don't even know anything.

I do my best to try and ignore him and rush straight towards a cluster of uniformed Border Force guys. Surely they'll act if this guy tries anything stupid?

I'm about ten feet from them, when the guy catches up and grabs my arm so hard it hurts.

CHAPTER THREE

"A moment, if you don't mind, Miss?" The man flashes a quick smile at me, but his eyes don't seem friendly at all as he towers over me.

I look down at his other hand to find some kind of official-looking ID in his hand with a big dark blue Metropolitan Police logo across top. Who is this guy? I glance up at the officers ahead of me but they're not even looking in my direction.

"Detective Clyde, Met Police Counter Terrorism Command."

His words make me pause to read his credentials again. I suppose it could be real, he's even got a metal badge-type thing attached to the other side of the leather ID card holder.

"Miss, you were seen earlier this evening with a person of interest in one of our investigations. It is of the utmost urgency that you tell me everything you know about this man." Detective Clyde takes his phone out of his pocket and shows me a rather grainy picture of the mysterious stranger in the suit as he's running along a busy road, across a fence next to some railway lines and finally, getting into the back of my car. They even have pictures of me behind the wheel. Damn! What have I got myself embroiled in?

"I… Well, I don't know the man, clearly, he just jumped into my car and made me drive him here. A person of interest in what exactly?"

"That's confidential."

"Ah." I stare down at my shoes, feeling rather stupid indeed.

"So you hadn't met him until today?"

I slowly shake my head, and look up at Detective Clyde's stern face again. Maybe I watch too much TV, but he doesn't look quite posh enough to be a detective. The other guy, though…

"What do you want to know?" I ask, blinking at him innocently—I hope.

"Where is he?"

"He told me he needed to stop some flight. Dangerous cargo, or something."

Detective Clyde lets out a frustrated chuckle.

"What if I told you *he* is the one with the dangerous cargo? It is imperative that we stop him before he gets airborne."

I shrug and shuffle from one foot to the other. Although the ID and the badge thing look real enough, there's something about this guy that rubs me the wrong way. From the crew cut blond hair to the scar on his left eyebrow, right down to the commando boots and cargo trousers, he doesn't look like much of a policeman. Then again, what do I know? If he was wearing a uniform, I may not have questioned his identity at all.

"Well if you know he's here, and you know he's trying to escape on some flight, why don't you just shut down the airport for a while as you catch him? Wouldn't that solve it?" I think out loud. The stranger's words about catching those responsible for intel still ring in my ear, but I'm curious what this guy will say.

"It's not so simple, disrupting the travel plans of thousands of people." He gestures around us at the crowded terminal. "We would prefer to resolve this matter more quietly if possible."

"That makes sense," I mumble.

"Now, if you don't mind coming with me," Detective Clyde says, while placing his hand firmly on my shoulder.

I shake it off instinctively. His touch feels inexplicably wrong. Then again, he did just bruise my arm trying to catch me, so it's no surprise I'm not up for more physical contact right now.

"Actually, I do mind. I don't know the guy, I don't know anything except what I've already told you, and I'd really like to get home. I have plans. A date."

"Miss, I'm afraid I can't let you go just yet." The detective's voice turns firmer, more determined.

I'm not sure how to react. Here I am, in the middle of a massive crowd and yet alone in my struggle with this scary dude who seems determined to detain me. After a couple of moments of indecision, the tannoy in the background breaks the silence between us. *Flight SV118 to Riyadh… cancelled…'* That's my cue, my signal that the mission has been successful as far as I'm concerned.

"Well you can't hold me against my will. Unless you want to arrest me without cause?" I ask.

"You'd be surprised what I can do." He glares at me, his eyes are cold as death.

I consider my options. I definitely don't trust this supposed policeman: if his version of events is true, then why did the flight get cancelled? But he's definitely not going to let me go.

The uniformed men are still in place relatively near us. If his badge is as real as it looks I can't count on them to help me though; they'll consider him one of their own and me a criminal. Meanwhile, the staff entrance door I saw Alec use earlier is only a short sprint away. I can only hope it's unlocked. It's my best shot.

"Fine. At least let me call my date to cancel," I say, looking him in the eye again. Eek. His stare gives me shivers.

He nods and instead of getting my phone from my pocket, I start rummaging in my bag until my fingers grasp the same item I had desperately clung to earlier today when I first came face to face with a potential threat. Lush Lavender, *not his style.*

In one swift move, I whip the bottle out of my handbag, while kicking down hard on his right foot, and spray my deodorant all over his face.

He lets out a surprised yelp, lets go of me to cover his eyes and I make a run for it without looking back. I've never been much of a runner—neither for sprints or long distance—but it's amazing what the human body can do when threatened.

Within seconds I make it to the door, twist the handle, and nothing happens. Locked. *Fuck*! I turn to see Detective Clyde rubbing his eyes, and the Border Force guys who have finally noticed the commotion have reached him as well to see what's what.

My heart is hammering in my throat and a cold sweat collects on my forehead as I try the handle again and again. Now what? Where do I go before the detective collects himself and comes after me? Then after one final tug on the door, it pushes open and I storm in, bumping right into someone so hard we both stumble inside as the door slowly shuts itself behind us.

"Whoa, I'm sorry. You OK?" I ask, while stepping back and taking a look at who I've just accidentally body-slammed. It's the guy—the mysterious stranger from my car. What a relief!

"Yeah, I'm great, you?" He grins at me, while propping me up with both hands. It hadn't struck me back in the car, or even when he got out and ran towards the cargo area, how tall and broad he really is. But now, face to face with him again, it's impossible to ignore.

My heart had been racing before, in my panic to get away from the scary detective outside, but now, I'm flustered for a whole new reason. I'm not sure how to react anymore, so I just nod. Fine, yes, it takes a lot more than bumping into a hot guy to hurt me.

"So you did it," I stammer, after taking way too long staring into his eyes. Green, honest eyes. "There was a guy, Detective Clyde outside. Wanted to hold me for questioning or something, but I ran."

"Clyde, you say? Jovial, somewhat rotund Scotsman?"

I frown at his question. No, that description is way off.

Before I can answer, the door behind us slams open wide and there he is, red-faced and even more menacing than he already looked before.

"Gotcha," Detective Whoever sneers.

Before I get the chance to react, I'm pushed backwards further into the corridor, as the sexy stranger positions himself protectively ahead of me. Oh shit, they're going to fight, aren't they?

I cower down behind a chair and table that's blocking part of the hallway, and peek up over it to watch the showdown. Punches fly, as the two men go head to head in full force. Detective Creep gets a couple of early hits in, but then the hot stranger has his vengeance and manages a powerful kick right into the scary guy's chest, throwing him back against the door. Sexy stranger surges forward, restraining the detective in sort of a stranglehold, making him struggle and twitch against the reinforced steel of the door.

He has nowhere to go.

"Who was behind all this?" sexy stranger asks.

The other guy doesn't respond, only lets out a muffled groan when the hold on his throat is tightened.

"Who's your inside man?"

I feel like I've somehow gotten stuck inside an action movie. It's surreal, exhilarating, and completely unlike how I thought tonight would turn out.

The scary man still doesn't respond. I shuffle around to get a better look when all of a sudden I bump against something soft, warm…

"Holy fuck!" I scream, seeing the slumped-over figure behind me, sitting in what is presumably a puddle of his own blood. I try to get up, stumbling over my own feet in the process and hit my head against the wall.

"Are you alright?" the sexy stranger calls out from behind me, but I can't answer.

"Nexus will prevail!" The detective's voice echoes through the hallway.

Is he dead? My heart is racing again, and I can't breathe. I feel like a woollen blanket is thrown over me, reducing my vision from the outside in until I see nothing but a blurry tunnel. Finally, even that slips into darkness.

CHAPTER FOUR

When I awake, for a moment I'm certain everything has just been a crazy dream. As the world comes back into focus however, I'm not only looking at the potentially dead guy from earlier, but also the detective who's collapsed into a similar heap nearer the door.

His eyes stare blankly at nothing, and there is white foam in the corner of his mouth.

"You OK?" A voice speaks in the distance.

I try to collect myself, get back onto my own two feet, but all I end up doing is flapping about on the floor like a fish out of water. My knees might as well be made of jelly, and my muscles don't have the strength to pick me up.

"Tess, calm down." The mysterious stranger in the suit comes into view as he kneels down in front of me, putting his arm on my shoulder.

"Easy for you to say," I pant, while shaking his hand off. "Are they… dead?"

"He is," the stranger nods over at the door. "The other one will be fine, don't worry."

"I'm not… Why? Why'd you kill him?"

"Believe me, it wasn't my wish for him to die, but as soon as I let go of him to check on you, he took something and died within seconds."

"Why would he do that?" I mumble, staring at the dead guy's face. *Shit, this image is going to haunt me forever, isn't it?*

"He didn't want me to know what he knows."

"But he's a policeman…"

"Believe me, that was not the real Detective Clyde." His voice is solemn, almost sad. I turn to look at him again to find his expression equally glum. "I can only hope he's not dead too. Nice man."

"Shit."

"Yeah."

"Now what?" I ask, looking over at the guy who according to Green Eyes *isn't* dead. Now that I'm calmer, I finally do see breathing movements.

"Once my partner arrives, I'll hand over the suspect for questioning, and I'll finally get to enjoy my day off."

"What about your unit? You said it was compromised or something?" I ask, while rubbing the side of my head. *Ouch.* I guess I hit it on my way down when I fainted.

"I've received word that the situation has been resolved. A leak, apparently, within our ranks. Looks like this guy here tried to infiltrate Scotland Yard as well."

"Ah." That's all I can manage to say. All of this is way too weird for me to come up with some clever or thoughtful remark.

"Tess." The suited stranger places both his hands on my arms. "Thank you."

"But I didn't even do——" Our eyes meet and I'm lost again. I shouldn't let this guy have such a profound effect on me, and yet… The way he looks at me suggests he's equally interested, even if I can't quite understand why a stud like him would even notice a girl like me.

I blink a few times, trying to shake the fuzziness in my head, as well as figure out if all this is in fact still a dream or hallucination, but every time I open my eyes, the green depths in front of me still invite me to drown in the fantasy. He leans down slightly, bringing our faces closer together. His breath tickles and teases against my skin.

He smells of a subtle aftershave or cologne, with a hint of something manly and rugged mixed in. When he reaches over and pushes a lock of my hair behind my ear, it takes my breath away.

I instinctively lean in closer, until the tips of our noses almost touch, tilt my head and wait. His hand, which had been resting on my shoulder so far, wraps around the back of my neck and pulls me in. I feel faint again, but not in a bad way this time.

Our lips touch and send shivers down my spine. His kisses are gentle, controlled almost, but this facade is quickly reduced to rubble when I part my lips, signalling my willingness for more. Our tongues find each other in a feverish embrace. I wrap my arms around him, feeling his hard, well-trained body underneath my fingertips.

Oh God, he's easily the sexiest man I've ever seen and now here I am, sucking face with him! It's all too good to be true.

A muffled moan originating from the bleeding man by the wall interrupts. Despite how it seemed, we are in fact still stuck in the real world, where I was nearly arrested by a fake policeman while he stopped a flight from taking off with some mysterious and dangerous load on board. I pull back, looking him in the eye again. What the hell are we doing?!

"I never did catch your name?" I finally ask.

He glances over at the man on the floor, who is stirring slightly, then makes eye contact with me again.

"Liam." His lips curl into the beginnings of a smile as he nods his head. "Liam Everson. At your service."

"Nice."

Before we get the chance to do or say anything more, the door opens, revealing an equally buff, much more rough around the edges guy in commando gear, flanked by a petite yet intimidating red-haired woman no older than forty in a tailored trouser suit.

"Everson. Good job, old boy," Commando guy says, while stepping over the dead fake detective. He winks at Liam before focusing on me.

The redhead cocks her head to one side and gives me a suspicious look as she enters.

"Boys, contain the situation, will you?" She nods at the three men still outside the door, all also clad in what looks like all black combat gear. They jerk into action instantly on her say-so. One checks the vitals of the two bad guys on the floor, another cordons off the area outside.

"Agent Everson. I expect your report on my desk by the morning," she says to Liam, whose amusement—although subtle—is still very obviously written on his face.

"Next time, try not to involve a civilian. Have her debriefed and include her statement in your report. Dismissed." Her eyes rest on mine for a moment, before stepping ahead into the corridor and bending over the bleeding, softly whimpering man. She grasps his hair, lifting his head to get a look at his face.

"Process him and take him for questioning, Clark, I want an ID ASAP, understand?"

The cheerful commando who had entered first nods his head. "Yes, Ma'am."

He gives Liam a slap on the shoulder and gets to work, while Liam takes my hand and leads me out of the corridor and back into the terminal. The area has been sufficiently cleared that we have space to exit freely, but there are still crowds of curious bystanders in the area, observing our every move.

"Wow. She's a ball breaker," I mumble.

Liam chuckles but doesn't respond, simply guides me through the commotion until we're well away from it all and once again nearing the coffee shop where I had waited initially. It takes me a few moments to realise what's happening.

"Where are we going?" I ask, looking down at Liam's hand still hanging on to mine.

"You tell me," he says.

"Well it's your day off and you're all dressed up." I glance at the black suit. Damn, he looks good in that suit. "Where were you going?"

"Dinner."

"Dinner? All by yourself?" I ask.

"Not anymore. Unless you have a better idea."

I'm not sure I'm hungry. Am I hungry? "Dinner sounds lovely." Though I'm not hungry yet… not for food anyway. "Or we could always skip ahead to dessert." Me and my big mouth, I blurt it out before I can stop myself.

Liam pauses and looks at me again, his eyes seem almost sparkly. "I like the way you think."

On the way to where I'd parked my car, we never let go of one another. We barely speak, just rush onwards, eager to get to where we're going.

I don't know what this means; is it a fling; a one night stand? Something more? Who cares. It's completely crazy and exactly what I want and need right now. Our kiss earlier had been full of promise, full of possibilities. I can't wait to see where else we can go tonight.

He pays for the parking, and I hand him my keys. Not sure why I do, it just somehow feels right and he doesn't object. Once we're out of the parking lot and on the road again, I can't take my eyes off him and as such am totally unaware where we're going, until at least half an hour later we pull up outside a fancy Georgian building.

We get out and he hands the keys to a valet, who stares at my crappy old car a bit too long before mumbling something and getting into the driver's seat.

"Good evening, sir, ma'am." A uniformed man tips his hat at us and opens the large glass door for us, allowing us to step inside the elegant marble-clad lobby.

Looking around, I'm suddenly glad to be still wearing my stuffy work clothes. Jeans would have been very much out of place in an establishment such as this.

A blonde with perfect hair nods and smiles at us from reception as we head towards the lifts. Liam knows exactly where he's going, he doesn't pause or hesitate as he leads us up to the fifth floor, suite 505, which opens with the help of a keycard in his hand.

"Welcome. Make yourself comfortable, I've got to make a call." He smiles at me, then turns around and heads into probably the bedroom, leaving me feeling a bit lost. The room is large, much bigger than the living room in my modest flat. The wooden parquet flooring is partially concealed by a massive Persian carpet, the colour of which perfectly matches the upholstery of the elegant sofa set. All of it looks way too expensive for a hotel room.

I leave my handbag on a shiny dark wood side table and take a quick round of the room, checking out the paintings on the walls. They look real, you can see the actual brush strokes, so they're not prints or reproductions it seems.

"All done. Now where were we?" Liam says as he steps back inside, his tie loosened, and top shirt button undone.

"Is this like a safe house or something?" I wonder out loud.

Liam laughs, then steps up behind me and wraps his arms around my waist.

"No, silly, it's a hotel."

Yeah, OK, I knew that.

"Not any hotel I've ever stayed at," I remark, trying to cover my embarrassment.

Liam leans down, letting his lips brush past my most sensitive spot on the side of my neck.

"If you change your mind about skipping ahead to

dessert, there's a room service menu over there on the coffee table," he whispers.

The tickle of his breath against my neck makes me weak. I shut my eyes and shake my head.

"Not going to change my mind."

"Good, I'd be heartbroken if you did." With those epic last words, Liam scoops me up into his arms and carries me into the other room. The bedroom.

CHAPTER FIVE

I can't stop staring at his beautiful face as he lays me down onto the bed. He tries to get up, but I keep hanging on with my arms tightly wound around the back of his neck.

"You're a beautiful woman, Tess."

His lips tempt me with every word he speaks. His eyes hypnotise me. I want to ask him why me, when he looks like the sort of guy who could get any woman he sets his sights on. But there's something in the way he looks at me that makes me swallow my doubts and questions.

He dives down into the crook of my neck, biting and nibbling on my skin until I can't stand the tickles anymore. Then he prises my hands apart and forces them onto the pillow either side of my face. He looks down at me almost like a predator, ready to devour me, and I cannot wait.

"Let me touch you," I whisper, while admiring his face, every inch of it. The fine laugh lines, which make him look so genuine, the full lips I already know the taste of.

He shakes his head and lowers himself onto me as he tugs at both my hands, making me stretch my arms above head level until my wrists can fit comfortable into one of his hands. Then he shifts his weight, allowing his free hand to start unbuttoning my blouse. Bit by bit, more of my skin is exposed. He traces along the edge of my bra, seemingly pleased with what he's seeing. Full cleavage, my best feature I think. Even as he reaches further down towards my belly button, his expression is one of fevered admiration.

He doesn't mind I'm not fit like him, that I carry a few extra pounds which I've so often wished away. If he does, he's not letting it show.

"Beautiful," he whispers, just before running his palm across my stomach, stopping just short of the waistband of my skirt.

I don't care anymore if it's an act, here's a man who knows how to make a woman feel sexy, despite herself.

"Your turn," I say, looking down at his still concealed chest. I want to - need to - know what's under there. Every indication is nothing short of spectacular. The men I'd been with in the past had probably never even seen the inside of a gym. Nobody had ever carried me to bed before - never even attempted it, that much I know. What other differences will I discover?

He pulls back, his lips curled up in a subtle smile. Without letting go of my wrists, he starts to unbutton himself.

My eyes are soon glued to the sexiness revealing itself to me. Well defined pecs, washboard abs, utter perfection. If I wasn't already on my back, I'd feel faint all over again. All this is mine for tonight? Am I the luckiest girl in the world or what?!

"Wow."

He takes his shirt off his free arm, then quickly switches hands to rid himself of the shirt entirely.

"You're very good at this. Keeping me in place," I mumble.

"You could say I have a lot of experience in confinement techniques." He leans down, his lips only half an inch from mine.

"Yeah, I bet," I breathe, muffled by his kisses. No more controlled teasing, he's ready to take things to the next level.

Our tongues meet again, fuelled by a renewed hunger for pleasure. His firm torso presses up against my soft curves, making me struggle desperately to get free. He finally does let go, allowing me to explore his body for myself. Flawless skin covers the mountains and valleys of his muscles. Warm, almost fiery to the touch, I pull him closer against me from his shoulder. His equally toned, perfect shoulder.

His lips move on down my neck, heading straight towards my cleavage, but without the impatience I'd grown accustomed to from other lovers. He takes his time, seemingly relishing the taste of my skin.

I start to struggle one-handedly with his belt, while teasing his shoulders with my fingernails. He shivers slightly, but doesn't pull away. As I make my way down his shoulder blade, my fingers find something different, unexpected. He freezes as I flatten my hand against his back to continue my exploration. His breaths quicken against the sensitive skin of my collarbone.

One, two, three scars. They're long, extending almost all the way across his otherwise perfect back. One criss-crosses the other two, as if he was whipped and his tormentor changed direction at one point.

His forehead rests against my chest, I can almost sense his heart racing more than before. I wonder what happened to him, but it would be wrong to ask, so I move on, hooking my finger into the waistband of his trousers and tug.

The moment of awkwardness passes, he recovers himself with a deep breath, leaning up again and wedging his hand underneath my back to reach my bra hooks. It doesn't take him more than a couple of seconds to undo it, and almost tear it off me.

The mischievous grin from before is back as he looks down at his discovery. Whew, back to normal.

I return his grin and undo the zip on the side of my skirt. He gets the hint and follows suit with his trousers. I've been shy before, with other guys, sometimes insisting the lights were off for our first time together, but with Liam, things are different.

He made me feel at ease before we'd even begun. Then just now when I found the scars on his back, I felt like somehow he let himself be more vulnerable with me than would ordinarily be the case. That's why he had held my hands above my head earlier, it all makes sense now.

Looking down at his completely naked form, I can't take it any longer. I want him, all of him, right now.

"I need you," I say, not caring one bit how clichéd and stupid I sound.

He leans over towards the bedside table and grabs a foil packet from the drawer.

"Yes, ma'am."

Then he's back on top of me only moments later, with my legs spread wide apart. I close my eyes as his impressive length nudges at my entrance. I'm ready, but then he reaches down between us.

His fingers tease and caress me as he continues to increase the pressure on my pussy. Oh God, I need him to get it over with, to go where only few have gone before. It's been a while, and I'm aching for him to take me as his.

"Please," I moan, as he continues his manipulation of my most intimate spot. It feels so good, and yet so inadequate.

For a moment he just seems to hover over me, I

can see him staring at me when I open my eyes again. Then, it's time. He lowers himself down, pushing against me harder until my lips part and he enters me.

I let out an involuntary gasp. He looked big before, now my body has confirmed it.

His eyes are shut now, little beads of sweat collecting on his brow. He starts with shallow, gentle movements, allowing our bodies to grow more comfortable.

I wrap my arms around him, pulling him down hard. He grinds down, filling me to my core. It feels amazing, despite the initial burn.

Every inch of my skin is highly sensitised and burning up. Especially my fingertips continue to crave contact with him, so I let my hands roam his body freely. Flawless or scarred skin, it makes no difference to either of us now. It's all good.

He speeds up, caught up in the moment as much as I am. Every thrust accompanied by a primal groan signalling his heightened pleasure.

Oh yes, that hits the spot! I angle my hips upwards, and marvel at the ease and fluidity of his movements. He leans up enough to shift his weight off me, then hooks his hands under my knees and lifts up my legs until they're resting on top of his shoulders.

I'm at his mercy, spread and helpless. His thrusts intensify, harder and faster he ploughs into me. His cock seems to grow with ever-increasing tension.

Although at first he was obviously in control, that's no longer the case. His discipline is fading, as his eyes turn dreamy.

"Liam! Yes!" I cry out, feeling the beginning of *that feeling* creep over me.

He's back, at least his green eyes are alert once more as he looks down at me, while continuing to fuck me. As gentle as things had started out, we're well past that and doing it rough and hard now. Just how one would imagine a guy like Liam would enjoy. No running out of steam at that most crucial moment, no early disappointments, just complete focus and attention on getting me where I need to be.

My leg slips off his shoulder and I lift up just enough to be able to reach him. My hand rests on the back of his neck, and he gives in and presses his whole body into me again. His muscles ripple in waves under my hand. It's amazingly beautiful to feel him move against me.

Our bodies fit together perfectly, hard and soft, strong and gentle, yin and yang.

The tickle in my lower abdomen grows exponentially, spurred on by his fingers which have found my nipple. Every touch of his is electric, while his cock manages to stimulate my depths better than anything I could do on my own - even with toys.

His movements don't show it, but he's getting louder with every thrust; riding the same wave I am.

I hear a scream, then realise it's my own voice. My fingernails dig into his arse, in one last effort by my body to not let him get away. He grinds his hips into me, sending me flying over the edge of control. Every part of my body is set alight, overwhelmed with pleasure.

His forehead rests against mine, when I finally have the sense to open my eyes, I see that his are tightly shut still. Our bodies are covered in sweat, but it doesn't feel dirty, instead it feels like a prize. An achievement.

In my own moment of passion, I didn't even notice he had his.

I don't want to let him go, and he's in no hurry to move. Time passes in slow motion. I focus on his breathing, try to bring my heartbeat down with his. Things I'd wanted to know earlier and shied away from seem less dangerous now.

"Why me?" I whisper.

"This is going to sound stupid."

I shake my head, his eyes are still closed but he can feel it because his forehead is still resting against mine.

"I saw you talking on the phone. Though I know I'd never seen you before, something clicked. I needed to get to the airport and I just knew that you'd help me. I had to find out why."

"Why?" I repeat.

"Why you seem so familiar. I had to know you." As soon as he finishes his answer, as crazy and irrational as it sounds, it makes perfect sense to me anyway.

I press my lips against his and am rewarded with a deep and passionate kiss the likes of which I'd never felt before.

Between my legs, I can feel his cock stir, ready for another go.

He grabs hold of my wrists and lifts me up along with him until we're on the other side of the bed: him on his back and me on top. I look down and smile, *I'm ready too.*

We keep going like this for what seems like hours, interrupted only by a short meal and the occasional cuddle break.

I'm old-fashioned generally, so I've never had a one night stand before. I never thought strangers could feel such a connection, to share such tenderness as well as lust. If that's what this is - a one night stand - I'll take it any day.

Later, countless rounds later, my body refuses to cooperate any longer though I suspect he could still keep going. He doesn't argue or even appear disappointed, just takes me into his arms. We talk, about nothing, about everything, about the crazy stuff at the airport. Just another day at the office for him, apparently. I can't imagine what that's like, the most excitement I've ever had at my own job was when that shrew Karen got into a shouting match with someone, who promptly quit on the spot.

"Must get home... Work tomorrow..." I hear myself say, just before I slip into a deep, content slumber with my head resting on Liam's shoulder.

CHAPTER SIX

Beep beep beep beep beep!

I hit snooze on the alarm and struggle to open my eyes.

What a crazy, wonderful dream I've had. Ignoring the nagging voice in the deepest part of my mind that a stud like Liam would never actually be that interested me, I close my eyes again for a rerun of every last detail of our time together. How the dim ambient light highlighted his amazing physique. Not an ounce of fat on the man, unlike my own body. The ease with which he carried me to bed. The passionate kisses, desperate moans, but most of all the mind-blowing pleasure we'd felt together.

Wait, where am I?

I shoot up and look around the dark room. The alarm sounded familiar enough. I blink a couple of times and sure enough outlines of furniture start to fall into place. I'm at home, in my room. Alone.

But how did I get here? As if nothing ever happened…

It had felt too good to be true, all of it. Even the scary parts of last night felt too movie-like, too surreal. There's a dull pain in my head, suggesting one of two things: the onset of a cold or a mild hangover.

Could it be that actually I ended up going out with Maggie and someone slipped something into my drink, causing all this craziness to unfold in my own mind? Could it all have been a trippy fantasy? No, it felt too real for that.

I fall back into my pillows, and close my eyes again. Ugh. I wish I could make sense of it all.

He got into my car, then we went to the airport, then, after he saved the day we left. Where did we go? A hotel. And yet now I'm here and he's not. Even though I don't remember getting home, I have a feeling that if I took a look outside the window right now, even my car would have made it back to its normal place somehow.

Unsure how to feel about last night, I decide I'd better just get on with my morning routine so I make it to work on time. After yesterday's appraisal, they'll do their best to find more faults in my work, and showing up late is not going to help any.

I stretch out my arms, before slipping out of bed. Weird, I'm even wearing my normal pyjamas.

It's only when I take the first step, that I get a clear sign that perhaps last night wasn't just in my head. My thighs are incredibly sore, like that one time Maggie convinced me to join her at her spinning class.

Images of last night come flooding back. How he had me on my back, my legs pushed up onto his shoulders, then spread wide. How I rode him a little later on, until I was so worn out I couldn't continue, so he took over, finishing both of us off.

I can't suppress a smile, even though there's no one around to see it.

Carefully, and without putting too much strain on my already aching legs, I make it through the living room and into the kitchenette. Everything's tidy, just how I left it, except in the middle of the counter, there's an empty mug with a piece of paper sticking out from underneath.

My heart starts to race as I pick it up and scan the unfamiliar handwriting.

Tess,

Last night was incredible. I hope you'll forgive me for taking you home and leaving you here on your own, but it's for the best. My life is complicated, as you may have noticed, and you'll be safer here.

Still, I need to see you again. What do you say: next week, same time, same place?

You have my number.

Liam

I fold the paper into half, and hang onto it tightly, smiling again.

Next   week,   you   bet   I'll   be   there!

PART TWO

CHAPTER ONE

I can't believe it's going to be another four days until I get to see Liam again. Time has slowed to a crawl, every day at work seems to last forever. How will I manage?

Sitting in my car, ready to head home, I can't decide quite what to do so I keep fidgeting with my phone, looking at nothing in particular on its blank standby screen. Perhaps I should just call him. But then, that would be needy, wouldn't it?

Some movement in the corner of my eye distracts. I could swear I saw something in my rear view mirror, but now that I'm scanning the office parking lot, all looks quiet. *Great, now I'm losing my mind as well.*

Instead of dialling Liam's number, I select Maggie's. She'd better be free tonight!

"Hey, Tess," Maggie answers, sounding as groggy as ever before her shift.

"Hey! Wanna meet up tonight? I'm all antsy and don't know what to do with myself. Make up for last Thursday."

"It's all that guy, isn't it? You're so screwed." Always the blunt one, Maggie tends to say the first thing that pops into her head without fail.

"Well… Yeah, OK, it's the guy. I can't stop

thinking about him. If you'd seen him, you'd understand," I try to justify myself.

"I still can't get over the fact that you actually spent the night with some stranger, who basically kidnapped you earlier that same night."

"He did *not* kidnap me!" I protest into the phone at full volume, before catching myself. "Really. He did *not.*"

"Well he did just get in and make you drive him around, while waving around a gun."

I sigh deeply. Maggie can be quite protective.

"Never mind that, I can handle myself." I wave her protests away with a dismissive hand gesture, even though she obviously can't see me through the phone.

"Uhuh."

"Are you going to tell me whether you're free to meet up, or not?"

"Not, I'm afraid. Can do tomorrow, though?"

I sigh again. *Balls.* Looks like it's *Friends* reruns and a sad, lonely takeaway dinner for me tonight.

"Sure thing, tomorrow, let's go for a movie or something," I suggest, trying to look forward to it despite the twenty-four-hour delay.

"It's a date." Maggie ends the conversation with a leisurely yawn as we say our goodbyes and hang up.

Now what?

I twist the key and listen as my car coughs to life. Again, a shadow or something makes itself known to me in the mirror, but when I turn around and carefully examine the backseat, as well as the surrounding cars in the lot behind me, all is clear. *What the hell? Why so paranoid?*

Shaking off the craziness, I put the car into reverse and pull out of my spot. Off to the right of the lot, I can see Karen's car. Karen's much newer, much nicer car. It occurs to me that I could just bump into it a little to get back at her for screwing me over last week. The scratches won't show on my old rust bucket, but it'll drive her nuts, I just know it. There aren't even any cameras inside the parking, only at the entrance and exit as far as I know.

Stop it, you would never do something like that!

I tighten my jaw, trying to swallow my residual anger as I drive past Karen's Ford without incident.

The road is clear enough to allow me to join it straightaway so I speed off, glad I don't have to see this place for another fifteen hours at least. As I pass through the familiar roads largely on autopilot, I wonder if Liam is out there somewhere, investigating or chasing bad guys or whatever it is he does on a daily basis. Perhaps he's out there getting into some other girl's car, flirting with *her* instead of me. *No! Enough already!*

I have got to stop thinking about him, or I'll have an accident. During the rest of the drive, I try to keep my eyes and thoughts firmly on the road ahead.

By the time I reach my neighbourhood, my stomach starts to remind me how little I've had for lunch. I decide to park up outside the local Chinese takeaway to get my regular Monday night Chow Mein fix. Thank God there's an empty space left, in between a van and the banged up silver sedan I recognise as the takeaway delivery vehicle.

Efficient as always, they have my noodles ready within five minutes and I head back out, keen to get home and tuck in. As I unlock my car, I hear the van doors behind me slide open.

Two hands grab me by my arms, pull me back and before I complete the shriek that started to pass my lips, something dark and musty is pulled down over my head. I don't get the chance to see my assailant.

"Calm down and you won't get hurt," a deep male voice whispers behind me, and something in his tone convinces me that he's serious.

What the hell?!

I just freeze in the dark, with my heart skipping a few beats. The food drops down beside me onto the pavement, making a muffled splatting noise, and my now empty hands are pulled back and tied up with something hard and thin, like a wire. *What to do? Run?* As if I'd get very far, even if I did manage to shake off the man's firm hold on my wrist.

He drags me backwards and lifts me up into what I assume is the back of the van. The door slides shut and I sink down onto my knees, landing on a pile of something soft. I don't even want to consider what it might be. Moments later, another click suggests one of the front doors of the van has been pulled shut, and soon after, the engine purrs to life.

Maybe I should have fought back, tried to get away? Instead I just gave up, like a complete coward. And it was just one guy, wasn't it? At least I only heard one.

The van reverses out of the parking space and breaks so hard I'm thrown over backwards onto more of whatever soft thing I'd felt earlier. Whatever it is, I'm glad it's there, cushioning my fall. The tyres squeal as the van races off, turning sharply to the right, making me lose my balance again.

Shit, I am so screwed.

I'm stuck, completely cut off from most of my senses with a cloth bag of some sort over my head, which smells of sweaty socks. That, and the fact that the van is throwing me left to right repeatedly is making me feel ill, until finally I curl up into a ball as best I can without the use of my arms.

Minutes that feel like hours pass, and I'm completely disoriented by the time the van stops moving and the engine is switched off. The resulting silence tries to deafen me, but then the door beside me slides open with the same ominous scraping noise from before. Wherever I've been taken, we've arrived and I don't have a clue how long we were on the road for.

Two hands grab my ankles so hard it hurts and I thrash about, trying to evade them. It's pointless though, all that's done is make the kidnapper's fingers dig into me harder.

"Stop messing about," the same voice growls at me.

I swallow hard, realising that perhaps I'm taking unnecessary risks. Perhaps my first instinct of just going along with whatever this guy wants from me is the safest bet. He drags me over the hard wooden panelling of the van floor, until my legs dangle out of door, then flips me over onto my stomach and lifts me by my arms.

My knees shake uncontrollably when he sets me down onto my feet. Shit, I bet my outfit is ruined. That's just perfect.

Try as I might, the sweaty bag on my head blocks out all light, until suddenly he yanks it off me. I'm blinded by what look like those super powerful spotlights you see on building sites, unable to see what's beyond.

Where am I? A warehouse? Whatever it is, it's big, judging by the echo when the kidnapper shuts the van behind me. I turn, hoping to get a look at him but he's dressed head to toe in black, including a mask concealing his features, even his hair colour.

He reaches out for me with gloved hands, and drags me by my arm towards one of those steel reception chairs you see in offices, a few feet away from the van. I stumble over my own feet on my way there, then am roughly pushed down into it. He fiddles with my restraint and opens it, giving me some relief from the dull ache that had started to develop around whatever wire it is he used to tie me up. But my respite is short-lived, because he immediately fastens my wrists onto the metal armrests of the chair.

"Don't try anything, you hear me?" he grunts.

I bite my bottom lip and wait, with the sound of my own frantic heartbeat filling my ears. *What does he want? Why am I here?* The man in black turns, then takes a few steps away, beyond the nearest spotlight facing me, making it impossible for me to see him, it's so blinding.

I want to scream, cry out for help, but I doubt anyone would hear me. And anyway, now that panic has taken hold of me, I doubt I could utter a sound.

"Tess Aldershot. I apologise for my associate's rough treatment of you, but good help is hard to find nowadays," a much calmer male voice speaks from beyond the spotlights. I forget to breathe, and threaten to choke on a stray droplet of saliva that's trying to head straight for my lungs, making me cough violently.

How does he know my name?

That means this wasn't random, but a planned abduction.

CHAPTER TWO   LIAM

"Goddamn it, Clark, this one's locked up tighter than the A4 on a Friday night." I straighten myself and look over at Clark's equally weary expression. The suspect in the interrogation room is turning out to be a lot more trouble than expected. Days and days of questioning have led nowhere. The only thing we seem to have worn thin is our own patience, not his.

"Stubborn bastards, these Nexus guys," Clark responds. "Hey, Everson, how about we try another tactic?"

"What do you suggest?"

"It seems they've scared this guy into silence, so we'll just have to convince him he has more to fear from us."

"All right. Bad cop, bad cop it is then." I give Clark a final nod before pushing open the steel-reinforced door leading to our cuffed suspect.

"You want to tell us again how it is you were found smuggling unauthorised cargo into the baggage hold of flight SV118?" I say, while placing my - unloaded - gun on top of the steel table in front of the terrorist.

The man looks at the weapon, blinks a few times and presses his lips together tightly while evading my gaze.

"We've got all night, and then all day. You haven't even been processed. Nobody will come looking for you," Clark responds. "You won't believe the amount of discretion we have when holding people like you."

"Only last week, there was a horrible accident with a suspect… One form. That's all the paperwork we had to fill out, and we're in the clear." I put my hand on top of the gun, caressing its smooth finish.

"Everything you think you know about human rights doesn't apply in this building. In fact, this facility doesn't even officially exist…"

The suspect looks up in shock, then stares at the wall on the far end of the interrogation room again.

"Please. They're going to kill my family," he stammers at last.

Finally, now we're getting somewhere. I let out a sigh of relief, but do my best not to let the man see it.

"In that case it's in your best interest to cooperate so that we can find the people responsible and ensure your family's safety. Because the longer you're in our custody, the more certain your buddies at Nexus will be that you've cracked," Clark says. We share a look, indicating we're both aware that we've all but won.

"Where did you get the package? Who ordered you to smuggle it on board?" I bark.

The suspect sighs, then hides his face in his hands.

"I never saw his face, only a silhouette. Said his name was Fletch."

"Fletch. So it's true," I whisper, mostly to myself.

"In the video, I could see my little girl tied up and crying. Fletch was standing beside her, but the lighting was such that I couldn't make out what he looked like really. Average build."

"Anything else? Anything you could recognise?"

"Just his voice. I'd recognise his voice anywhere."

Damn. I try not to let my disappointment show. In all the time we've been investigating Nexus, and its figurehead, the mythical Fletch, this is the closest we've come to identifying who are involved. And still, we're no further.

In my pocket, the familiar buzz of my phone is vying for my attention. Mine is an unlisted number, so the only calls I get are from a very select few. It's almost always important.

I turn towards the door, with my hand slipping into my pocket.

"What's going on? Where are you going?" The terrified voice of the suspect calls after me.

"Relax, we'll investigate your claims," Clark says.

"What about my family?" the man asks.

"Do you have a copy of that video?" Clark retorts.

While the two of them continue their back and forth, I make it to the corner of the room and check the screen on my mobile. Unknown number. *Strange.*

"Hello?" I answer.

"Agent Everson. I believe I've got something that's very dear to you. Someone, rather," a peculiar male voice says. Nasal, as well as particular, how he pronounces every syllable very carefully. The background is suspiciously quiet, no ambient noises, no hiss of a bad line or iffy mobile signal. Something about this call seems off.

"Who is this?" I ask.

"You already know," the voice answers. "Say hello, why don't you, darling."

"Uhh… Liam?" a choked voice says. *Shit.* That sounds a lot like Tess! So while I'm trying to find out more about the ghost we only know as *Fletch* from our suspect, the devil himself phones me up. How ironic.

"Are you OK?" I ask. A cold sweat erupts all over my body as I realise what's happened. How could I not have seen this coming? I've been so busy trying to find out more about the airport incident, that I don't consider they could change strategy and go after Tess.

"Who are you talking to?" The scared man behind me interrupts. "Shit, tell him I didn't say anything. Tell him not to kill my family!"

"Shh!" I hiss, while gesturing at him frantically to keep his mouth shut while keeping my finger on top of the microphone towards the lower edge of the mobile phone.

"If you want to see her again - alive - you'll have to do a little something for me, Agent Everson." Fletch's voice sounds as if he's grinning. Clearly a narcissist, so proud of his own cleverness.

"What's that?" Though I'm no stranger to having my own life endangered, I've never had to deal with a threat to someone I care about. That's why this unit hires people like Clark and me. No family, no attachments, nothing to lose.

"My associate, who succumbed to an unfortunate cyanide poisoning at the airport. He had something on his person that's of value to me. Bring it to me, and only then will you see the girl again."

"What? Where?"

"X marks the spot. You'll receive further instructions momentarily."

"I didn't say anything. I don't know anything," the suspect sobs behind me, making me close my free ear with my finger to reduce the distraction. "Please save them. I'm so sorry."

A click marks the end of my conversation with the criminal mastermind, Fletch, and my attention is immediately diverted back into the here and now, when I hear Clark shout something unintelligible, followed by a struggle.

Just when I turn fully to look at what's happening, I see the man, his hand covered in blood spewing from a wound in this throat where he's managed to wedge in a ballpoint pen I assume he's taken from Clark.

"What the fuck? How did he get that pen?"

"Took it right out of my pocket." Clark steps back, holding his hands up as though trying to distance himself from the horrible scene in front of us.

"Jesus Christ, I turn my back for one minute!"

"That was Fletch, wasn't it? On the phone?" Clark squints his eyes and looks at me suspiciously.

"None of your business," I snap, still shocked that we indeed managed to lose a suspect in this room, like we'd threatened the man with earlier. It'll be a lot more than one simple form to resolve this one though. Then it occurs to me that *we* didn't lose a suspect at all, *Clark* did. And he doesn't look as horrified as he should be.

"If it's related to the case, it's very much my business." Clark faces me, with his hands on his hips.

"It was the girl from last week. She's in a spot of trouble and needs my help," I explain, while maintaining eye contact with Clark. He's good at spotting a liar, here's to hoping I have the skills to fly under his radar.

Why is he so keen to press me for information? And how come he doesn't care someone just killed himself with his pen? How do I know I can even trust Clark at all? It wouldn't be beyond an organisation like Nexus to plant a mole deep inside the anti-terrorism unit itself. That seems like exactly the kind of play a guy like Fletch would make.

"I've been wondering about that girl, what was her name? How did she end up involved?" Clark asks. "A friend of yours?"

"Not quite. I'd never met her before that day."

"Right." Clark takes a step forward, looking me up and down. "You seemed quite… *Familiar…*"

I shrug, careful not to let my suspicions show. "We clicked. So what?"

"I just don't get it."

"I didn't ask for your understanding. I don't stick my nose in your private life, do I? Anyway, the fact is, she's called for my help, and I'm afraid there's a bit of urgency to it, so I'm going to go ahead and leave now."

"What about this?" Clark nods his head towards the dead guy.

"Don't ask me, that's your pen sticking out of his throat, you handle it. I'm sure it'll resolve itself once the boss lady reviews the surveillance footage of the interrogation. Nothing to worry about, right?" I ask.

"Right."

I shove my phone back into my pocket, glance at the dead suspect, then Clark one last time and exit the room.

Wow. If Clark indeed is involved, or even if he

isn't, I sure hope he doesn't come after me and jeopardise everything. *X marks the spot,* Fletch had said. I'm going to have to examine the body of the guy from the airport, and I can't afford to have an audience when I do.

This could get messy, but I know it's what I have to do. I wouldn't be able to live with myself if something happened to Tess which I could have prevented.

I navigate my way through the corridors, making sure I'm not overlooked as I head for the autopsy room.

HQ is quiet most days; field agents - as their name suggests - tend to spend most of their time out in the field. Only the most bare bones back office staff stay behind here. And of course the pencil-pushers at the top. It's only because of the interrogation that Clark and I are even at the office today.

I do a quick scan through the round window in the door; the clinical white examination room looks to be empty. I swipe my badge to release the lock, while already trying to formulate a suitable justification for my presence here in case the logs are checked later. It all depends on what I find inside. What Fletch wants me to exchange for Tess's safety.

Once inside, I don't need to look far for the body. The refrigerated air, combined with the sight of the dissected cadaver on the main plateau in the centre of the room, give me the shivers. *There he is.*

I step up closer to the dead man. His expression is calm now, disguising the violent manner in which the poison took his life at the airport. One might think he was asleep, except his chest cavity has already been sliced open, and some organs removed and sent off for analysis as part of the autopsy.

His arms are placed neatly along his side, and only now do I get a look at the intricate tattoos covering his shoulders and upper arm. Multiple black bands of geometrical shapes, are twisted and wound together in a pattern reminiscent of a Celtic knot. I follow the pattern up and down his arm with my fingertip, instinctively looking for Fletch's clue.

Then I see it, surrounded by swirling bands of ink, an unmistakable 'X'. I pick up the scalpel from the tray beside the body and make a small incision. With the help of a tweezer from the same tray, I prod and poke around inside the wound I have just created until I find what I'm looking for.

The small metal plate comes out cleanly, thanks to the lack of bodily fluids in the carcass. I hold it up closer to the light, to get a better look. It's some kind of electronic chip.

Just as I put it down onto a piece of paper towel, ready to carry it with me, my phone buzzes once in my pocket, startling me. That'll be the instructions.

Tess, hang in there! I'll be with you shortly.

CHAPTER THREE

"X marks the spot," the mysterious man in charge says. "You'll receive further instructions momentarily."

Although I only heard half the phone conversation, I understand that this will put Liam in a difficult position. He has to deliver something to this man in exchange for my safety. I'm sure whatever it is will be something Liam's superiors would not want to get into the wrong hands, so in doing what my captor demands, he'll be going against his orders.

Would he do that, for me? I want to believe that he would, but what if he doesn't? Or what if he tries but fails to reach here somehow?

"You'd better hope your *boyfriend* follows through," the nasty masked man from the van snarls at me, strengthening the fears I already have anyway.

He pulls out an almost comically large knife, holding it up close to my face. Comical, if only it wasn't potentially going to be used on me. I press my lips together tightly in a desperate attempt not to scream.

"Now, now, there's no need for that. She's our guest now," the calm voice, who had just been on the phone with Liam, says. "And she won't be any trouble. Will you, dear?"

I shake my head, and breathe a sigh of relief when the mean guy puts the knife away again.

"Agent Everson should be here shortly," the calm voice reassures me.

I strain my eyes against the bright lights pointed at me, trying to decipher something - anything - about my captor that may help later on, if I do indeed get out of here. The silhouette of the man moves ahead of one of the lights, enabling me to see his outline much better, even if his features are still obscured.

Average height, average build, neutral accent. Great, that doesn't narrow things down at all. He's wearing a hat, like an old fashioned gangster, so I can't even tell how he keeps his hair or what colour it is.

He reaches behind himself, pulling at something, which makes a horrible screeching sound as it drags over the concrete floor. A chair. He sits down facing me and folds his arms.

"Tess, darling, do tell me how you found out about the incident at Heathrow last week."

Shit, he's trying to interrogate me. So he thinks I know something, only, I don't!

"I… Liam said he needed to get to the airport," I stammer.

As much as I hate telling this man anything at all, especially about Liam, I'm just hoping that giving him titbits of information which he already knows anyway will buy me time. If Liam is indeed on the way with whatever it is this man wants, I may just be OK.

"Right. Specifics would be good."

My throat feels tight, making it difficult to speak, but I do my best to explain anyway. "I swear, I don't know anything else. Liam got into my car and said something was happening at the airport."

"He just got into your car and told you to drive? You don't expect me to believe that, do you?" The man sounds a little less reserved than before, there's a hint of impatience or frustration in his voice.

"That's what happened." My heartbeat has sped to a frantic pace, making me feel faint again. I blink against the bright lights, but they continue to blind me and I still can't see much of my interrogator. The darkness beyond the lights gives an oppressive, claustrophobic effect.

"So you're trying to convince me that you and Agent Everson aren't working together?" The man fidgets with something, perhaps his pocket, then lights up what looks like a cigar. The glow from the lighter and then the cigar tip is just enough to illuminate his nose and his lips. He's white. Again, that doesn't narrow things down much.

"No! I mean, yes! We don't work together. I work in a call centre in Brentford!"

"Right you are." The man shifts his weight in his

chair and crosses one leg over the other, then takes a deep drag from his cigar. "An excellent front."

"Front? No, I actually work at a call centre. I'm in the customer service division for Cellnet!" I exclaim. Damn, he thinks I'm lying to him. If I can't convince him, who knows what he will do to me? Then again, if he hurts me, I won't be much good as leverage to make Liam give him what he's after, will I? Surely he can't be planning to hurt me!

"So it was just a coincidence Agent Everson got into your vehicle that day?"

"Yes, that's exactly right. I'd never even met him before that day." Although that does sound quite thin, even I have to admit that.

"And when my man at the airport tried to foil your little plans, you just happened to evade him. Coincidentally, not because you in fact recognised his name and knew it wasn't the real Detective Clyde…" The man shakes off his cigar, without ever turning his head away from me. Although I can't see his eyes, I can feel his stare and it's making me more vulnerable.

"Uhmm…" I shudder at the memory of the fake detective at the airport. There was something creepy about him even before he showed his true colours and fought Liam. Thinking back, his voice sounded similar to the guy from the van. Maybe the rough accent, or just his tone.

"And it wasn't your plan from the beginning to

lure him into the staff area, where Agent Everson could eliminate him.”

“He didn’t! He said the guy killed himself!”

The silhouette in front of me lets out a laugh and sits back. “He killed himself, you say? Why would he do that?”

“I… I don’t know.”

“Well then… Perhaps you’ll change your mind once you’ve had time to think. My mother always used to say ‘nothing promotes clarity like a little rest’.” Before I get the chance to respond, the man gets up from his chair and vanishes into the shadows.

The horrible guy from the van steps up beside me and stuffs that same smelly old bag over my head again. The musty scent makes my stomach turn.

“Nobody lies to Nexus. We always find out,” he whispers in my ear.

My throat goes even drier than before. If I don’t come up with something more useful to say the next time the main guy questions me, who knows what will happen to me? I can only hope Liam will turn up soon enough and resolve things.

Once again, I’m alone in the dark. It occurs to me that I can’t recall the duration of the drive to get here. Neither do I know where Liam was when he got the phone call. How long until he could reach me? How long have I even been here already?

In the background, I hear footsteps, voices.

Except for the main man with the strangely calm voice and the one who kidnapped me, I had no idea there were others here. It makes sense though.

With the bag still blocking my view, my other senses seem heightened. I listen on as they drag some large object over the concrete floor, then a bunch of them huff and strain, presumably to pick up whatever it is. It must be heavy.

The van doors that had held me captive earlier slide shut and the engine starts. Way behind me, a motor jumps into action, possibly to power a loading bay shutter and the van drives off until I can hardly hear it anymore. There is a moment of eerie silence, before the same motor starts to whine again, presumably to close the shutter once more.

Damnit, Liam, how long are you going to take?

CHAPTER FOUR   LIAM

The address they sent to me turns out to be a warehouse near Stanwell. As it is set away from the village itself, as well as the Heathrow boundary, I'm certain my presence will be detected as soon as I get near it. I park up at the side of the road a little away from the facility and find my binoculars for a better look.

The place gives the impression of being abandoned, there are no cars parked outside on the overgrown concrete parking lot. The shiny video surveillance system installed along the mesh perimeter fence suggests it's not unused at all, and extremely well secured inside.

There is no way I will be able to sneak in unnoticed. If I call for back-up or try anything funny, Tess will die. The message had said so and I already know Nexus tend to make good on their threats in these scenarios.

The only solution I see is to go in, as they instructed, and surrender myself, but first I need to secure the package. My fingers wrap tightly around the small metal tube in my pocket containing the chip. I twist the cap open, and empty it into the ashtray of my car. Hopefully nobody will think to look for the chip there.

After putting the binoculars back into the glove box, I slip a small collapsible knife into my shoe just in case. I take a deep breath and open the car door. Although I'm going to play along with their plan, I'm not going to make things too easy for them.

I walk up towards the main entrance of the facility. As soon as I'm within range of the first cameras along the fence, I take the empty metal tube and hide it in the weeds growing along the pavement. Then I head directly for the gate, climbing over the top as instructed.

Nothing seems to stir inside the building. The blacked-out windows betray no movement, but I'm certain Fletch's people are in there somewhere, watching me. I head for the front door, reach out for the handle. It creaks open before I get the chance to touch it.

"Welcome, Agent Everson. Please come in," the same voice I'd spoken to on the phone says. The slight echo suggests he's using some kind of intercom system, but the voice is unmistakably the same.

"Where's Tess?" I ask, while waiting for my eyes to adjust to the pitch black inside the warehouse.

Clever, how he's trying to disorient me.

"Patience, Agent, you'll be reunited shortly."

I take a couple of steps toward the voice, and the door creaks again, clicking shut behind me. Now I can't even benefit from the daylight coming in from the door anymore. I try to find my way by touch, taking another few steps ahead while reaching out for who knows what with both arms. It's no use, there's nothing there.

A moment later, two hands grab hold of my arms, force them behind me and tie them with what feels like a zip tie. The person pats me down, making sure I've come in unarmed as instructed, then steers me ahead, further into the dark. My instincts tell me to fight, but since Tess's safety is at stake, I resist this urge.

"The package?" Fletch asks. The echo of this place makes it impossible to determine where Fletch is by sound alone.

"I have it," I say.

"Well then, hand it over!"

"I have it, but not *on* me," I clarify. "Let me see Tess and I'll tell you where it is."

Fletch sighs. Footsteps echo in what must be a huge empty space. It did look like a warehouse from the outside, and the sound quality in here suggests I've entered right into the middle of it.

"All right then," Fletch says, sounding a bit further away than before.

The invisible man - or men - holding me, shove me forward, prodding me in the back whenever I pause.

"Liam?" I hear Tess calling out for me. She sounds muffled, distant.

"Don't worry, I'm going to get you out of this," I try to reassure her. There's no response. I don't give myself the chance to worry, to let fear take hold of me. I'm completely focused on finding some way - any way - to ensure her safety.

With a loud click, a couple of spotlights are switched on, pointing directly in my face. Like a deer in headlights, I freeze instinctively, but the person restraining me relentlessly pushes me ahead, nearer to the lamps, until they make my eyes burn.

"There. Satisfied?" Fletch asks. I squint and strain my eyes to see what's ahead of me.

"I can't see. Where is Tess?" I say.

I shuffle ahead further, as the man behind directs me. Then I finally see her. A woman, tied to a chair with a black covering over her head, surrounded by yet more spot lights. She's only about twenty feet from me, and yet she seems completely out of reach.

The sight of her in such an undignified position fills me with anger, but I swallow it, knowing that losing my temper won't help either of us right now.

"Tess? Is that you?" I call out.

The woman stirs, lifting her head in my direction, even though she probably can't see anything through the dense fabric blocking her face. "Yes, Liam?"

I'm so glad to hear her voice. So relieved she's

actually here. That means there's hope of getting her out of this yet. Otherwise Fletch might have just hidden her somewhere else, or killed her already.

"Now. If you don't mind telling my associate here where you've kept the package." As soon as Fletch finishes his demand, a man steps out in front of the light, clad all in black. Even his face is covered by a black balaclava, hiding his features completely. All that's visible is the menacing look in his steel-grey eyes.

"Outside. I've hidden it," I say.

The man pulls another chair out of the darkness and gestures at it. "Sit."

Something about him seems familiar, his voice perhaps, but I cannot place it.

I obey though, taking a seat, and the hands that had kept a firm hold on my arms until now loosen just a bit as the restraint around my wrists is cut.

They'll want to secure me to the chair now too, obviously. Then they'll want to get the package and verify it, before possibly killing the two of us right here. I can't let that happen.

I flex my muscles, preparing myself for a fight. The man in black steps around me, holding a couple of black plastic ties. The hands on my arms have relaxed enough for me to slip out from underneath their grasp. I turn around and punch the man who had been holding on to me right in the gut, making him double over.

The man in black with the zip ties pulls a huge knife from a thigh harness and charges at me. I jump up from the chair, pick it up and fling it in his direction, in an effort to distract him.

The lights are still bothering me, making it hard to see the two men I'm fighting, so I focus on sounds instead. Sometimes it's easier to visualise a fight with your eyes shut, acting only on instinct. And anyway, if I can't see properly, neither can they.

Footsteps off to the side remind me that Fletch and who knows how many other people are still around, hiding in the darkness. They'll have guns, and if I get shot, Tess will definitely die as well.

I dodge the guy in black again, narrowly avoiding his knife and see an opening to punch him swiftly in the throat. He goes down almost instantly, and the large Rambo knife makes an almighty ruckus at it falls to the ground beside him.

The other guy is still doubled up on the floor, with both arms wrapped around his abdomen. In just a split second, I reach down, remove one of my shoes, as well as the folding knife. Keeping the knife in my left hand, I fling my shoe hard at the light, blocking my view of where I assume Fletch was. It falls over with a loud clatter and shatters, giving my eyes some relief at last.

I sprint towards the other light, and use it to scan

our surroundings. I can't see anyone, especially Fletch. He must have made an exit as soon as I started to resist.

Then a loud whimper makes me turn around towards Tess. She's no longer alone.

A man - Fletch, presumably - has wrapped his arm around her throat and is holding a gun to her temple. His black fedora hat is obscuring his face, all I can tell is he's quite unremarkable in terms of build, and most likely Caucasian.

"Another move and she's dead, Agent Everson," Fletch hisses.

It's peculiar how his voice remains mostly calm with only subtle undertones revealing how he really feels. I'm sure he's livid, but he still sounds completely in control of himself.

"Kill her and you'll never get your chip," I respond.

He presses the gun against her head harder, making her cry out. She must be terrified. The realisation that all of this is my fault stabs at my insides. Focus!

"It'll be OK," I say, to reassure her as well as my own frazzled nerves.

Adrenaline is coursing through me as I grip the knife in my left hand tightly. It's so small when folded, he probably hasn't spotted it yet.

I slowly raise my other hand, as though I'm

surrendering.

"Wait. I'll give you the chip and you give me the girl, OK?"

"No sudden movements!" Fletch warns me.

I fumble with my left shirt pocket, opening the button on the flap and then pretend to reach inside with my left hand. Before he's able to see what I'm up to, I quickly transfer the knife into my right hand, while continuing to rummage around in the pocket for the non-existent chip. Then I remove my hand, grabbing hold of a bit of fluff from the shirt fabric between my forefinger and thumb, and hold it up ahead of me.

This is when the spotlights turn things in my favour. There's no way he'll be able to make out what I've got in my hand without coming closer.

Fletch looks up, straining to see whether I've actually got what he wants, and relaxes his hold on Tess's throat. *This is my chance.*

Just as I'd practised in training so many times before, I quickly flip open the knife, and throw it straight at him. The sharp blade pierces his eye, making him stumble backwards.

He screams, the gun falls to the floor with a loud, echoed clang, and I charge ahead, reaching Tess and Fletch within the blink of an eye. I grab the knife, and force it in further, beyond the crunch of bone, right into his skull. He stops screaming as his limbs start to twitch.

I focus my attention on Tess now, who is softly crying into the black cloth bag.

"Shhh… It's OK," I say, while freeing up her face, using the dirty cloth to wipe my bloodstained hand.

Big, tear-stained eyes look up at me, making me melt inside. What is it about this girl that she can make me feel this way? I've always liked the company of women, favouring to keep things casual as most guys I know do, but never like this. I've never felt *normal* around any of them.

"They thought we worked together. They didn't believe me when I said that we didn't. I thought they were going to hurt me if I didn't tell them anything else. How did they know my name? Who are these people?" Tess rambles, then pauses and simply stares at me in silence for a moment. "I missed you."

It's my fault. All of it. I put her life in danger by involving her last week. Although I missed her, I can't find the words to respond to her, so focus on the task at hand instead.

I lean over behind her chair, pull the knife out of Fletch's head, and wipe the blood off before using it to cut through Tess's restraints. She wraps her arms around me tightly as soon as she's free, clinging on to me for dear life. I may have just rescued her, but her embrace makes me feel like I'm the one being set free. Will I ever get used to how she affects me? I hope not.

"Holy shit, that's disgusting!" she exclaims, as soon as she spots Fletch's dead body behind her chair. "People keep dying whenever we're together!"

I'm not sure why, but something in her tone makes me chuckle. At least this time, she didn't faint.

"Let's hope this is the last time that happens," I remark, though something tells me it's not. People ending up dead is an occupational hazard I thought I'd gotten used to by now. Her involvement changes everything.

CHAPTER FIVE

I'm still terrified, my heart is hammering in my throat and my knees are jelly, and yet I'm thrilled to see Liam again. I just wish it were under different circumstances…

Forcing myself to look away from the horrifying image of the dead guy in the gangster hat on the floor, I instead opt to just look at Liam's face. He rescued me. Again.

"Where would I be without you? You totally saved me just now," I mumble, looking into his eyes again.

"Probably at home. Safe," he remarks dryly.

Fair point.

"At home, bored, more like it," I respond. Although the entire kidnapping experience was obviously terrifying, part of me is actually serious about the 'bored' remark. I haven't had this much excitement in my life, ever. And that's not entirely a bad thing.

"Now what?" I ask, looking around. Everything's as dark as it was before, so I'm still not able to see a thing.

"It seems strange that Fletch would have only two guards here. We'd better make ourselves scarce before reinforcements arrive," Liam says.

I let go of him, and take another look around the darkness. He takes my hand and points towards God knows what to our left.

"The exit is that way, follow me."

I do so without protest, eager to get out of this horrible place.

"What did the creepy guy want from you? I hope I didn't get you in trouble?" I ask, as we rush through the blackness and straight towards hopefully a door. My eyes are starting to adjust to the lack of light, but I still can't make out much around us.

As soon as we reach a wall, Liam starts to tap his hand along its width to find the way.

"Are you sure it's this side?" I wonder out loud.

The creak of a doorknob being turned breaks the silence, removing the need for him to respond.

"My car is outside," Liam says, while gesturing at me to exit before him.

He places his hand on my shoulder as soon as we're outside. Dusk has already set in, and the streetlights provide an eerie orange glow outside the strange, overgrown compound we've found ourselves on.

We head straight towards the main gate, which looks impossibly tall. It's secured with a large chain and lock. He can't possibly expect me to climb over?

I swallow my concerns when he offers me his hands as a step up.

"Don't worry. It's easier than it looks, just put your toes in the gaps and hold on properly," he says.

Somehow - I don't know how - I manage to make it all the way to the top. He climbs up after me and swings his leg over the top, offering me his hand to help me do the same and head back down. Amazing. I would have never thought I could do this!

"What's funny?" he asks, when we find ourselves safely back on ground at the other side of the gate.

"Nothing." I look over at him as he scans the surrounding roadside for any sign of danger.

So focused, so determined. The slight crease between his eyebrows makes him look so serious.

I've always scoffed at movies relying on creating a damsel in distress scenario to make the hero seem more impressive, but even I have to admit it's very sexy to actually get rescued. Or perhaps that's just because I already like him.

He looks different today, not in a suit but wearing normal clothes. Black jeans and a fitted dark grey t-shirt. Very simple, but oh so hot anyway.

"My car is just over there," he says, nodding at the unassuming black sedan parked up on the side of the road.

We rush over while he continues to keep a look out all around us. Then he gets into the car as soon as I'm in, turns the key and speeds off. It doesn't seem to matter where he's taking me, so I don't even ask.

All I want to do now is to just sit in the passenger seat next to him, my hand on his thigh. He holds on to it, in between gear changes. Neither of us seem to feel the need to talk, but the silence isn't awkward.

After spending the best part of ten minutes just getting my heart rate under control, I do at last start paying attention to our surroundings. The route looks familiar, we're getting close to my neighbourhood.

When he turns into my road, I finally do decide to ask; mainly because the prospect of him just leaving me at home and vanishing without a trace is getting me anxious all over again.

"You're dropping me home?"

Liam pulls into an empty parking space outside my building and turns to face me. His expression is quite cold, practical. Even though we're sitting next to each other in a confined space, still he feels miles away.

"After the day you've had, perhaps you should rest," he says, as if it's the most logical thing in the world. He's right, probably, but I feel anything but logical.

"You realise they picked me up outside my local Chinese, right? And they knew my name. What if there are more of these people out there, they could just turn up at my house."

I wet my lips nervously, anxious for him to change his mind. I desperately need him to stay. And it's only partially because I'm worried someone will come for me again.

He considers my justification for a moment, looks out the window as if to check the area for any threats, then focuses on me again. His eyes linger on mine, then on my lips for a bit. The tension between us is suddenly too much to bear, rendering me breathless.

"I suppose it would be safer for you not to be alone. Would it be OK for me to come up?"

I try not to make my relief known, but I'm sure it's written on my face anyway.

"That would be great." I smile at him, and he seems to relax a little at last.

We exit the car and head up to my flat. I try not to consider how much of a mess it is inside. *How does it matter, he's already seen the chaos that is my home when he dropped me off last week.* By the time I unlock the front door, my idle concerns make way for excitement. It's been a while since I've invited a guy home with me, and what a catch he is.

I look over at his face as I push the door open. He's staring at me, rather than at everything else around us. Something about him has changed. He's open again, available. Gone is the cold, business-like Liam who had taken over earlier to get us out of trouble. The man I see following me inside my living room is all warm, hot even. His eyes betray the passion that had haunted me for the better part of a week after our first night together.

Earlier it had seemed like he wanted to keep things professional, but now his defences are down again.

As the door squeaks shut behind us, he cups my face and presses his lips against mine, taking my breath away all over again.

"Did you mean that earlier?" he asks.

"What?" I breathe.

"That you missed me?"

He actually looks concerned, like he's not at all sure how I feel about him. It's endearing.

"I was being serious, no need to laugh at me," he says, while maintaining eye contact.

I only stop grinning when he lifts me up into his arms, effortlessly. This will never get old. I wrap my arms around him and nibble on his neck as he carries me into the bedroom.

"It's just funny, because normally that's the type of question I'd ask," I explain, looking into his eyes as he lays me down on my pillows.

"It's a pertinent question." He gets onto the bed half on top of me without ever breaking eye contact.

"It is."

He pauses for a moment, waiting for me to say something more, but the sight of him so near me is so distracting, the right words don't come to me just yet. Then, he looks down at what I'm wearing. I wait for a remark, but it's not forthcoming.

I gasp when he tears my clothes off me. Normally I'd be annoyed, but the outfit was already ruined after my earlier ordeal in the van anyway. And I've never had a man tear my clothes off before: that's the sort of thing that happens to perfect-looking people in movies and romance novels, not to girls like me. Only, right now, it *is* happening to me.

At least one of us is perfect…

He looks at me with fiery eyes, like he could devour me right now, no matter what or who stands in his way.

"I missed you so much, I thought I was going to go crazy waiting a week to see you," I whisper.

"Good thing we ended up seeing each other today then," he growls, just before diving down into my cleavage for further kisses.

"Yeah. Perhaps I should get kidnapped more often," I joke.

He pauses for a moment and leans up, looking me right in the eye again. "Don't say that. Something could have happened to you today."

"But it didn't, thanks to you."

"Right, but what if I'd been late? What if something had gone wrong? I wouldn't be able to forgive myself if I let something happen to you."

I press my lips together tightly. I don't want to consider what might have happened, only what's happening right this moment. He looks so sad, so conflicted. Here I am, on my back, half naked at his hand, and yet he seems more vulnerable than me.

"I can't explain it, I really can't." He sighs, and looks down at my lips, tracing their outline with his fingertip. "Tess, there's something truly special about you. Like you make the world a better place just with your existence. I've seen a lot of things most people don't get to see. Terrible, dark things. In you, I see only light. Does that make sense?"

I consider his words, the honesty in his emerald eyes. "It does. I feel the same."

He smiles briefly, there's something bittersweet in his expression. I wrap my arms around him and pull him down against me, desperate to shake the gloomy subtext in his words. Now I understand why he gets weird sometimes. He's got baggage, how could he not with a risky, dangerous job such as his. That's fine, I've got my own.

Tonight none of that matters, all that matters is how our bodies fit together, complement each other, how our minds find the beauty in one another. How I can make him forget about all the horrors in his world, and he can make me forget about the drudgery in mine.

He fumbles with his zip, and I quickly wiggle out of my panties, and struggle to unhook my bra, worried he'll tear that off too. Then he spreads me wide, and enters me with an urgency I've never seen or felt before.

We're in a rush to give ourselves completely to each other. Like anything could happen: the world could suddenly come to an end and we would be left wanting. Like life is too short, too precious to waste.

I run my hands over his back, feeling the scarred ridges I'd found during our first time together. Maybe one day he'll tell me what happened to him, or maybe not.

He thrusts into me repeatedly, each stroke sweeter than the last. His hands roam my curves, his lips taste my soft flesh. Everything about him, about us is perfect right now. Tomorrow, we may not be so lucky.

As little droplets of sweat start to collect on his brow, so do they accumulate on my forehead. But it doesn't matter, we're comfortable with who and what we are right now. I guide his lips towards mine for further, deeper kisses.

Sometimes the first time is the best, because the expectations created by that initial flurry of hormonal emotions cannot be met again. With us, the second time is even better, because we know each other more now. I hope this trend continues with the third, fourth and I-don't-know-how-manyeth.

I buck upwards to meet his feverish rhythm, my hips joining his in their quest towards relief.

They say violence and sex go hand in hand. I'd

never thought about it before, but now I know that they do. As scared as I was earlier, and as horrified when I saw the body of the guy who orchestrated my kidnapping, all those negative emotions have vanished and made way for passion unlike I've ever felt before.

A similar thing had happened last time. We ended up sleeping together even though one might think all the terrible stuff that happened at the airport would have killed the mood. The opposite had been true.

As Liam speeds up towards the final crescendo, heightening my own pleasure with every move, I dig my fingernails into his back. He closes his eyes, as do I, just focusing on the in-and-out, the fluid and regular movement of our bodies as we fight towards a common goal: release.

He freezes first, his body turning rigid in my embrace. I shudder upwards against him one last time, letting my body take me over the edge and down into the abyss of pleasure.

His forehead rests against mine, his rapid, strained breaths tickle my lips. The corners of my eyes burn, and almost straight away I feel the heat of tears streaming down my cheeks. Even if I wanted to, I couldn't do a thing about it.

He lifts himself up slightly, running his finger over my wet cheek.

"Did I hurt you?" he whispers.

The concern in his voice makes me cry even more,

but they're not tears of sorrow at all.

"No," I say. "They're happy tears."

He smiles at me, gives me a peck on my forehead and lifts himself up and off me.

"Sorry about this, but I've got to call in what happened. Before they get panicky back at the office."

I nod, then lie back to enjoy the remainder of the post-orgasmic fog I find myself in.

Before he gets the chance to get his phone out of his jean pocket on the floor, a loud crash rips through the quiet of my flat, and the rays of flashlights light up the half-dark interior. I let out a loud shriek, but it's soon drowned out by another voice.

"Anti-terrorist squad! We are authorised to use deadly force. Surrender now and no one will be harmed!" A man so loud he has got to be using a megaphone barks.

I instinctively pull my blanket over myself, while Liam just straightens himself and lifts his hands above his head. He doesn't even seem to care that he's naked, neither do the half dozen or so armed men entering my bedroom, led by the guy I remember Liam referring to as *Clark* last week at the airport.

"Clear!" Clark shouts, "Everson. Fancy seeing you here."

"Clark. What a lovely surprise." Liam leans to the side, nodding at the scary redhead who has also entered the room. "Ma'am."

"Agent Everson. Care to explain what happened today? Or should I arrest you for treason right now?" the woman asks.

"I'm sorry for this, Tess, I'm sure they'll repair your front door…" Liam says, while Clark puts a pair of handcuffs on him.

I'm lost for words, gobsmacked. Why the hell are they arresting him? Isn't he one of them? And he actually took down the guy who abducted me too, which is a good thing, right?

"I apologise for the intrusion," the red-haired woman in charge says to me, as Liam is led out of my room, and then my house by Clark and the other men. "And I'm sorry he's involved you in his treachery."

I look at her, then at the men who are leaving, and at her again.

"Liam rescued me," I mumble. "Why is he in trouble for that?"

"I'm not at liberty to say." The redhead gestures at the last man, standing just behind her like a bodyguard, and they both turn on their heels, heading straight for the door. "Have a nice evening, Ms. Aldershot."

PART THREE

CHAPTER ONE

All night I've been a nervous wreck. Is Liam OK? Surely it was all a misunderstanding, right?

My calls to his number were met with a *switched off* message. By five am, I am too exhausted to stay awake, and too frazzled to get to sleep. Maggie will have just reached home after her shift, so I call her instead.

"Hey, Tess, what's going on?" Maggie sounds alert concerned, obviously, why would I call her at this ungodly hour unless something was wrong?

"I don't know! I'm freaking out."

"Calm down, tell me everything," Maggie says.

I take a deep breath, then tell her everything that happened yesterday, from start to finish. Ordinarily I would have embellished details, or omitted things that may reflect badly on Liam, but by now, I don't have the mental capacity or patience for any of that. Maggie is going to get the whole story, warts and all.

Once I'm done rambling, she remains silent for a moment.

"You still there?" I ask, worried that perhaps the line has gone dead and I'll have to tell the whole story all over again.

"Yeah, just… thinking."

"I'm just so scared. What if they don't believe him? What if they keep him locked up?"

"Just so that I'm certain I've understood… These are *his own people*, who barged into your flat, invaded your bedroom while you guys were in the middle of some hanky-panky, and then they cuffed him and took him away." Although her recap is worded like a question, her tone sounds more like she's just making a statement.

"Right."

"And his phone is switched off."

"Right."

"Well… I don't see how there's anything else you can do. You have no way of contacting these people, you don't know where they're based. If they want to hear your side to clear things up, they'll have to be the ones to get in touch with you."

Maggie makes sense, as she often does. Of course that doesn't mean it's what I want to hear right now.

"He saved my life twice, Mags."

"You wouldn't have needed saving if he hadn't got you involved in God knows what."

I sigh. And that's exactly why I tend to filter the stuff I tell her.

"Either way, it's five-thirty in the morning, you've got a job to go to in a few hours. Afterwards we'll hang out and talk some more. Oh and I hope you don't mind, but Alec may drop in at some point, I thought it would be nice if you two could meet, finally."

"Sure," I answer absentmindedly.

We say our goodbyes and I'm alone again. She's right, I can't do anything. I put the phone down and fall back into my pillows. When my alarm goes off, it feels like only a minute has passed, not two hours.

———◆———

"Bye, Tess!" Karen's cheerful voice grates at me as she leaves for the day.

Meanwhile, my eyes are burning due to lack of sleep and I've got the lucky job of staying behind and finishing what should have been *her* work. Stupid reports. Stupid people. Stupid life.

I continue to grumble to myself while selecting various cells full of meaningless numbers in the stupid spreadsheet I've been working on for the better part of the afternoon. Just when I'm ready to throw in the towel and give up on it all, my phone buzzes once. A message.

My heart starts to race. Could it be?

Dear Tess, I apologise for last night, ever since we identified a mole in our unit last week, everyone's been quite paranoid. That said, last night taught me that our lives are and always will be incompatible. I am sorry. L

I'm not sure what to do, fling the phone at the wall and watch it break into a million pieces or scream until my vocal cords rip themselves apart. All day I've been waiting for some sign - any sign - to let me know that Liam is OK. And now this?!

What if someone else messaged on his behalf? What if it's a ruse? I take a deep breath, and hit the little 'call' icon beside his name.

It rings once, twice, thrice, and then finally there's an answer.

"Hello?" A voice answers. It sounds like Liam, but then, I've never spoken to him on the phone so how would I know.

"Tell me you didn't mean that?"

The silence that follows is painful.

Finally, Liam takes a deep breath on the other end, before responding. "Twice I've endangered your life. They're right, in our line of work, we can't afford relationships. It gives the bad guys leverage they shouldn't have."

"But…" Wait, who was right? Don't tell me the bitchy redhead is giving him relationship advice now.

"What if I hadn't reached you on time yesterday? What if they'd hurt you, or worse, killed you. I couldn't live with myself."

"Wait…"

"That's how people end up dead, Tess. You said it yourself. Whenever we're together, people die. I'm not about to wait around until one day you're the one who's killed."

Click.

Tears are prickling in my already sore eyes, and I feel empty as empty can be. Like my guts have been ripped out and dumped on the floor in front of me and there's nothing I can do about it. *No way. This is fucking unbelievable!*

I dial his number again, but this time there's no answer.

Great, just bloody ignore me without giving me a chance to have my say. *Men!* Always think they fucking know what's best for everyone else.

I shut down the spreadsheet, not giving a damn whether I'll get into trouble for not finishing it. It doesn't matter. Nothing matters. In another surge of rebellion, or recklessness, I turn the PC off by switching off the power, rather than doing it *the proper way.* I need to get out of here, right now!

Maggie will know what to do, even if it's just to watch girlie movies and drink wine together. And ice cream. We'll need ice cream.

I pick up my stuff and rush out of the office, straight to my car. I can't think of anything, focus on anything other than that pathetic excuse for a conversation I had with Liam just now. It's a miracle I make it to Maggie's place in one piece.

Rather than ring the bell downstairs, I slip inside

her building just as someone else leaves, and head straight for her door.

"Mags, open up, it's me," I shout, while banging my fist on the plastic finish door - the types you often see in cheap housing from the early nineties.

When it unlocks, I'm surprised not to be faced with Maggie, but a flustered-looking Alec. Shit, she had said he'd be coming over too. Crap.

"Hi. Maggie is just taking a shower," he mumbles, while eyeing me suspiciously. "I'm Alec."

I'm about to comment on his stares, when I realise that I've probably been crying, meaning my mascara must have run down my face, and the lack of sleep will have made me look half dead anyway.

"Hi. I'm Tess," I say, while shaking the hand he's offered and avoiding eye contact with him.

He waves at me to enter and I follow him inside. Maggie's house is a mess as always - a cosy mess, as she likes to say. We take a seat on the sofa, in silence.

"So… you're Maggie's best friend?" Alec starts, a painful few seconds later.

I just nod. I'm not up for small talk, or generally in a sociable mood after everything that's happened in the past twenty-four hours. If he thinks I'm an arrogant bitch because of it, so be it.

We don't talk anymore until a bathrobe-wearing Maggie enters the room, with a towel wrapped around her head.

"Tess, when did you get here? So you two have met then. Good." She walks around the messy coffee table, and I get up to give her a hug.

"Jesus, you look like shit."

I try not to cry again, but my face contorts itself into an ugly frown anyway. "I called him. Finally."

"Right… and?" Maggie sits down between Alec and me and puts her arm around me.

"After I've worried about him all night and day, no explanation, nothing. He's calling it quits. What the hell is wrong with men?" Realising Alec is still sitting there on the other end of the sofa, I lean forward, acknowledging his presence for a second. "No offence."

"None taken," Alec mumbles.

"He what?! The fucking nerve!" Maggie exclaims.

"Right? I don't know what to do anymore."

"You're here now, and that's what matters. Alec, would you be a dear and make us a cup of tea? We have a bit of girl talk to do," Maggie says.

Alec mumbles in agreement, he's clearly uncomfortable with the situation as it's about to unfold and glad to get the chance to escape the drama for a while.

We watch him leave before continuing our conversation.

"Now, don't spare any details. What did he say?" Maggie says.

I tell her the entire story, showing her the text message he'd sent first, and then recount our phone call word for */word, including how he didn't even give me the chance to respond to any of it.

"It did sound like him, right?" she asks.

I nod through the fresh tears. *I think so.* Considering he did refer to something I'd told him when we were alone, I'm pretty certain it must have been him.

"You know how I felt about the guy, right?" Maggie gives me a big hug, as I continue to sob into her clean bathrobe.

"I thought he was different. That you were just being paranoid," I complain.

"The whole thing from start to finish had alarm bells going off in my head," Maggie says.

I guess she's right. I can't find the energy to argue anymore.

"There's some ice cream in the freezer, let's get it out and see if we can find some ridiculous romantic movie on TV," Maggie suggests, as she's just about to get up.

"Wait, I'll get it. You go get dressed in the meantime." I lift myself off the sofa, stretching out my shoulders which have completely locked up, and reluctantly drag my tired body towards the kitchen, while trying not to bang into any furniture on the way. Meanwhile, Maggie stirs as well and disappears into the bedroom, shutting the door behind herself.

"Hey," I call out while opening the kitchen door, then pause when I hear his hushed voice inside.

"Look, I'll be free in a short while," Alec whispers. He hasn't noticed my presence or heard me call him.

I push the door open a little further, seeing him with his back turned in my direction, holding his phone against his ear.

"If the package is on the way to Folkestone already, we have nothing to worry about... Uhuh. Yes... And the agent himself? Right, so he'll be there in a couple of hours, tops. Perfect timing."

Remembering the weirdness at the airport last week, when Alec all of a sudden ended up manning the check-in desk of the flight Liam was trying to ground, formerly dormant suspicions are once again aroused. He blew off a date with Mags to *work*. That's just plain weird. And as far as I'm aware, Maggie and Alec don't even do check-in duty normally.

Now he's talking about packages, agents... What the hell is going on?

"All ready." Maggie's cheerful voice makes both me and Alec jump. "How about that ice cream?"

CHAPTER TWO   LIAM

"So you want us to believe that you managed to overpower two of Fletch's men as well as the mastermind himself in some warehouse in Stanwell?" Mrs. Hill - the boss lady, or H for short - looks like she has even less of a sense of humour than normal. The stark surroundings of our interrogation cell don't help matters any, neither do the handcuffs around my wrists. Following our standard operating procedure, they'd kept me awake all night but not started questioning until my patience had worn thin in isolation, many hours later.

"Send a team in if you don't believe me," I say.

"Why didn't you call for back-up?" Clark asks.

I eye him, looking for any sign that he is in fact playing for the wrong team. I can't believe how quick they were to take me in, while completely ignoring the fact that our most valuable witness from the airport died in Clark's custody yesterday.

Of course I shouldn't have kept Fletch's threats to myself, nor should I have removed the chip from the dead suspect in the morgue and taken it to Fletch's hide-out. But what other choice did I have? There's a definite rat stink hanging around this unit, and until I could be sure whom to trust, what was I supposed to do? Let Tess die?

"Fine." The boss lady dials a number on her phone, all the while keeping her eyes fixed on me. "134, Stanwell Moor Road. Beyond the reservoir?"

I nod in agreement. Yes, beyond the reservoir.

"This is a matter of extreme urgency, you understand? I'll expect your report within the hour."

"So where is this chip now?" Clark asks, leaning forward onto his elbows, which are resting on the steel interrogation room table.

"May I have a word, Ma'am?" I ignore Clark's protests, and keep my gaze firmly on H instead.

"Fine. Clark, I'll call you back in if I need you."

He reluctantly leaves, while I watch Mrs. Hill take a seat in the chair Clark had just vacated, across from me. She crosses her legs and waits.

"In private," I say, gesturing at the camera in the corner of the room.

She sighs and leans forward, switching it off with the button installed at the side of the table. Normally that's where I sit. Normally, I control those cameras, while someone else is in my chair.

"The chip is safe."

"Where is it now?" she asks.

"Soon, the other team will reach the warehouse and verify my story. Rather than waste time questioning me about some non-existent connections to Nexus, let's put our heads together and figure out who could be the real mole in our unit," I say.

She squints at me, pressing her lips together tightly, like she does whenever she disapproves of something.

"I'm listening."

"Yesterday, Clark and I were questioning the witness from the airport. After days of steely silence from his side, we were finally making progress, when all of a sudden the guy ends up having Clark's pen stuck in his throat. Coincidence?"

I wait to give her the chance to let my words sink in.

"I received the phone call from Fletch - at least I presume it was - and Clark was all over me. Who is it, where am I going, what's happening. It was rather suspicious."

"I see."

"And he seems awfully keen to get his hands on that chip himself. And was he the one who alerted you when I left the office yesterday? He had no way of knowing where I was going, so how did he know I was lying to him?"

"It's a theory worth exploring, certainly. If you let me know where the chip is, we can have it analysed and find out what's so important about it anyway."

"Agreed," I say, then tell her about leaving it in the glove box of my car.

"Thank you, agent. Now, there's still the matter of

the civilian. What do we know of her involvement?"

I shake my head. "Not involved. No way. We crossed paths last week completely by coincidence. I picked the first car I could find in moving traffic on the A4."

"I see. And then you involved her. I don't need to repeat myself and tell you what a reckless and stupid idea that was, do I?"

I take a deep breath. Tess. My heart wants me to think about her some more, but my current predicament means it's less than practical. She'll be worried sick about me by now.

"If she's indeed just an innocent bystander in all of this, your contact with her was the sole reason her life was put in danger yesterday. You understand this, don't you?" Strict as ever, H crosses her arms as she stares at me. Her tone is almost like a headmistress, telling off a bad student.

"From now on, you can't afford to make these kind of mistakes. Excuse me." She nods at me and gets up to make another phone call. I may not like what she had to say about Tess and me, but she's right. I knew it instinctively at the airport, but yesterday took things to a whole new level. Assuming she'll be satisfied when she retrieves the chip and gets confirmation from the team at the warehouse, I'll be back to work within the day. But I can't just go back to how things were... Not if it means putting Tess into even more danger.

"Everson's car. Glove box." She pauses, and just for a moment, her expression breaks from her usual cold, controlled demeanour, into something looking like panic. "What do you mean *it's not here*? I'd ordered for it to be retrieved from that girl's house, when we picked up Everson last night! Don't give me excuses, find the bloody car! What does the tracker say?"

H cocks her hip and rests her hand on her side. "All right. I understand. Stay on it."

"Agent Everson. Any idea what your car might be doing on the M20, heading for Maidstone, Kent?"

I shrug. Now it makes sense how they ended up at Tess's house last night; of course there's a tracker in my car.

"Maybe ask one of your boys who participated in your little home invasion last night?" I remark.

Although I have no idea what's going on, or why my vehicle is on the move, the outcome can't be good. What's on the M20? Where could it be heading? There's nothing there but fields, and ferries, and...

"The tunnel," I whisper.

"What's that?" Mrs. H demands.

"That's the only thing that makes sense. Nexus is planning to hit the Eurotunnel! And they want to make it look like I did it!"

"That's ridiculous. You're in custody, so you obviously couldn't have," she protests.

"True, but the general public and the media don't know I've been arrested, neither will there be any records to prove it. Occupational hazard of working for an agency that operates largely without official orders... I bet that they've prepped my car with plenty of evidence to point my way."

H's heels click loudly against the concrete floor as she walks around the desk, towards me. She unlocks my handcuffs and hands me back my work phone.

"You're restored to active duty. Agent Jenkins will be your remote back-up. Follow the tracker, and I'll dispatch another team to the Eurotunnel directly in the meantime. We can only hope that we'll make it in time, whoever has your car has had quite a head start."

I rub my sore wrists and give her a nod. Now things are personal. After yesterday's kidnapping went seriously wrong for Nexus, they're out for blood. And what better way to punish an anti-terrorism agent than to implicate him in what could very well be the worst terror attack in recent history?

Rushing through the empty corridors and down the stairs, I dial Jenkin's number without even slowing down. "Jenkins. What's the traffic situation like?" I ask.

"M25 clear for now. I'll open the hard shoulder

for you. Keep your sirens on when necessary."

"Got it. Keep me posted on where the target is."

I grab the first car key off the hooks in the booth next to the underground parking garage, then make my way out, pressing the button on the remote until I spot the flashing lights of the vehicle I'd randomly picked. Within moments, I'm strapped in behind the wheel and speed out of the garage and onto the main road with lights on and sirens blaring.

While I do my best to dodge the much slower traffic on my way to the motorway, I dictate a quick message to Tess. It hurts to think about, but I can't afford to endanger her further. I may have killed Fletch yesterday, but it seems like someone else has taken over control of Nexus seamlessly, planning a retaliation in less than twenty-four hours even! That kind of efficiency is what we've come to expect from Nexus. It was naive to think that with the death of Fletch, all that would come to an end.

She won't be happy. Hell, I'm not happy about it either.

I instruct the phone to send the message after hearing it read back to me and making sure it says all it needs to. Seconds later, it rings.

"Hello," I answer, dreading the conversation we're about to have. I do my best to stay on course, to not let my emotions question the decision I'd made. It's for the best if I cut all ties now, before either of us gets too involved… It'll hurt less.

With every word I have to fight the urge to close my eyes and to wish I didn't have to do this. I'd agreed to give up all this for Queen and country, but somehow that choice seemed easier before meeting Tess. Before feeling what I'd felt when I was with her.

The second time it rings, I know I can't answer because I'll falter. I'll change my mind… No, I must stay on track and figure out what's going on. I must do my job.

CHAPTER THREE

"Yes, I was just getting the ice cream." I try to justify my position just outside the kitchen door.

Alec looks at me suspiciously, but I ignore him and walk straight to the fridge, opening the freezer door. "Rocky Road, lovely," I remark, while picking up the heavy tub.

Maggie gives me a wide smile as I hand it to her, along with a couple of spoons.

"Say, you guys carry on," Alec says. "I don't want to intrude."

Shit, now what? He's up to something, I just know it.

"OK, sweetheart. That's very nice of you," Maggie says, while stepping up to him and giving him a big hug.

Think, damnit!

I just watch them as they exchange a quick peck on the lips. Instead of leaving straightaway, he makes his way towards the bathroom and I seize my chance to have a word with Maggie.

"Mags. Last Thursday he was supposedly sick, right?" I ask.

She turns to face me with one eyebrow in the air.

"What do you mean supposedly?"

"Well, he was at the airport. I saw him."

"No way!" she calls out.

I raise my hands in a calming gesture to make her keep her volume in check.

"I wasn't sure at the time because I'd only seen him in the pictures you'd showed me, but now I am sure. He was there."

"So?" She juts out her chin in defiance.

"You work the same shift, but he was already there, working. Don't you find that a little weird?"

"Maybe he covered for someone, wanted to get some extra money?" she suggests.

I shrug, maybe…

"Do you ever work the check-in desks?" I ask, while looking suspiciously at the closed bathroom door.

The boy is certainly taking a long time in there, but for once, that's a good thing.

"Never. Check-in desks are handled by airline staff."

"OK, well, he certainly seems eager to get out of here right now, I think you owe it to yourself to investigate why that might be. What if there's someone else?" I feel bad misleading her like that, but she'd never go along with my plan if I didn't stick the knife in her deeply.

"Oh, how dare you!" Maggie's eyes pierce me, shooting daggers.

"I'm just saying. It's worth checking out."

"And you want to what, follow him?"

"It beats sitting around at home shovelling ice cream into ourselves."

She pauses for a moment, thinking things over, then looks at the bathroom door and back at me.

"OK, fine. I just hope I'm not going to regret this."

As soon as she finishes speaking, the door opens and Alec walks out, smoothing his hair down with his right hand. *He's fucking involved, I know it!*

They hug goodbye, and he's out the door, leaving Maggie and I behind. I nod at her and grab my handbag. She shoves her phone into the pocket of her jeans and signals that she's ready. We open the door as quietly as possible, in case he's still hanging about.

The coast is clear, so we rush down the corridor leading to the lifts which are always out of order, and the staircase. There are footsteps down below us. Alec, presumably. He's talking on the phone again and I pause to be able to hear better.

"So he's on the move? Good. I've booked the nine-fifteen pm train. With a bit of luck the cameras will catch him just before it leaves, then, fifteen minutes later: boom. It won't take them long to implicate him."

Maggie is about to comment something, but I gesture at her to zip it. If he hears us, we're screwed.

"Right on. Nexus will prevail!" Shortly after Alec's final greeting, a door opens downstairs and the sound of footsteps fades away.

I can hardly contain myself and grab hold of Maggie's arm.

"Ouch," she complains.

"Shit, this is massive," I stammer.

"What? Who is Nexus?"

"Have you not been listening to anything I've told you earlier? Those are the people Liam was after!"

"But… I thought we were following him because you said there was another woman!" Maggie puts her hands on her hips and gives me an angry stare. "Explain yourself!"

"Look, I overheard him in the kitchen and got suspicious. There's no time to get into it now, but something's going down and I have a feeling it has something to do with Liam."

"What do you care? The guy dumped you!"

"Yeah… but…" She has a point, but I can't shake the feeling that something horrible will happen if I don't act on my gut feelings with Alec. Something irreversible.

"No buts, I think you're losing your mind," Maggie says.

"I don't have time to argue. I overheard Alec say something about the nine-fifteen train from Folkestone. What's in Folkestone?" I demand.

"The Eurotunnel."

"Exactly." *Holy shit, they're planning an attack on the tunnel.*

"So?" Maggie argues.

"So what would some evil organisation want at the Eurotunnel?" I wait impatiently for a response.

"I don't know, Tess, what would they want?"

"You heard Alec: boom! Blow it up! This is fucking serious and you're standing here arguing with me over who dumped who!" I rant. "Look, I have to call Liam. I don't have time for this."

Maggie waits while I get my phone out and dial his number again. Busy signal. Goddamnit.

"Shit."

"He's ignoring you, isn't he?"

I shoot her a nasty look and tap out a quick message instead.

Overheard phone call about Nexus attack on Eurotunnel. My best friend's boyfriend, Alec-something is involved. On the way. T

Send.

Then I race down the stairs with Maggie hot on my heels.

"Now what are you doing? Where are you going? Come back?" she calls after me.

"Gotta go. I'll see you later," I shout back, as I exit

her building and head straight for my car. I know it's risky, stupid even, but I have got to do *something* about all this! They may not have mentioned him by name, but it's obvious they're trying to pin this whole deal on some agent. I'm pretty sure it'll be Liam.

He did kill their figurehead at the warehouse yesterday, so they're bound to be out for revenge. It all makes perfect sense.

I twist the key in the ignition and my car coughs to life. Just as I pull out of the parking, I see a frazzled Maggie appear, waving her arms. Sorry, but I can't waste any more time. Liam needs my help, and I'm determined to be there for him. If nothing else, it's payback for saving my life yesterday.

After quickly going through all the options in my mind, I pick what I assume will be the fastest way to the M25. It's just past rush hour, so the roads are slightly quieter already, allowing me to make good time, filtering in between slower vehicles. Speed limits are for suckers, they mean nothing to me right now, neither does the risk of more speeding points on my licence.

I make it to the motorway in record time, hitting the ramp at sixty-five mph already. As soon as I can see clear ahead, I put my foot down all the way on the gas, and milk every last bit of power out of my tired old engine.

There is still a fair bit of traffic, as there always is

on the M25, but there are plenty of gaps for me to go through. Gone is the fatigue I'd felt earlier, gone is the helplessness. I have a goal now, and failure is not an option.

My phone rings and rings, but I don't dare answer it while going this fast. It's probably Maggie, trying to convince me to turn back.

———◆———

LIAM

I'm boxed in by cars front and back, all making their way through the roadworks at a snail's pace. The only release for my impatience is with nervous taps on the steering wheel. I've never been claustrophobic, but this gets pretty close right here.

Sure, the speed limit is fifty mph, but usually there's always some arrogant BMW driving bastard who thinks he's above the law, racing through much faster. Not today, though. Today, when actual lives depend on me reaching Folkestone at a decent time, everyone chooses to obey the limit.

"Jenkins, any way around this mess?" I bark into the phone.

Jenkins pauses at the other end, all I can hear is the tapping of keys.

"Afraid not, Everson. But you're halfway already,

then the road opens up again."

I sigh and disconnect the call. Damn.

Then it buzzes again, once. A message. I take a quick glance at it. Attack on Eurotunnel, tell me something I *don't* know. Wait, who is this from? *Tess?!*

I do a double-take on the message, reading it more carefully this time. This girl has a talent for finding trouble!

I want to tell her to turn back, not to get involved, but she doesn't answer her phone. After trying for five, maybe ten minutes, I see the end of the roadworks up ahead. Jenkins was right, the traffic does open up almost immediately.

Time to fly, so that hopefully I can resolve the mess at the tunnel before Tess gets anywhere near it. The last thing I need right now is for her to be anywhere near Nexus people. They're obviously trying to punish me for what happened yesterday, and if they can get their hands on Tess, they won't hesitate to kill, perhaps even torture her.

I grip the steering tightly until my knuckles show white, and speed up as much as the car allows. Lights on, sirens on, and hopefully everyone gets out of the way quickly enough. I'm about an hour away from my target at this speed. There's no time to waste.

And so I push on, dodging the occasional Peugeot driver going at fifty-five in the fast lane, hitting the M20 soon after. Thankfully all is clear up ahead and

I'm making good progress.

Jenkins checks in occasionally with updates about my car's signal. It's now at the Channel Tunnel check-in area and has remained stationary for the past twenty minutes. I don't stop to wonder why it hasn't been loaded onto a train yet, presuming that that's what Nexus has planned. I'll have to see what happens when I get there.

If I get there on time.

CHAPTER FOUR

The road is clear for the most part, throughout my drive along the M25, as well as the M20. Similarly, luck was on my side in that today's excursion came one day after my regular once a week trip to the petrol pump, meaning I didn't need to make any stops on the way for fuel.

By the time I see the boards for the Channel Tunnel, what was previously a warm, clear day, is turning cloudy and ominous. A sign of things to come, perhaps?

The wind is picking up, the trees lining the motorway cheer me on with their swaying branches. The sun has disappeared behind a big, grey cloud.

I wonder what Maggie must be doing now. I'll have to make things up to her later, whenever she's calmed down.

And Liam… I've had nothing better to do for the past hour or so than to think about everything that's happened so far. From worry, to anger, back to worry again, my emotions have run the entire spectrum today. He may have let me down, but some little part of me still wants to believe that things can work out. Otherwise, why am I here? I'm doing this for him, right?

I pull into the motorway exit towards the tunnel, and only now realise that I have no plan whatsoever. I'm about to reach my destination, and I have not the faintest clue what I'm going to do there!

It's not very busy, meaning there are only about four cars ahead of me at the entrance. I guess I'm going to have to get a ticket on the spot. Do they do those? Fuck.

"Hello, welcome to Eurotunnel. How may I help you?" the bored-looking man inside the booth says.

"Can I get a ticket for the nine-fifteen train, please?" I ask, while nervously fumbling with my wallet. *Shit. How much does a ticket like this cost?*

"Just a moment, I will have a look… Yes, there is still space on the nine-fifteen, but you don't have much time, meaning you'll have to go straight through to the check-in. Single?" He looks down at me impatiently while I rummage around in my bag, looking for some form of payment.

"Hmm?"

"Single or return?"

"Uhh… Single."

"That'll be seventy-three pounds, please."

I don't have that kind of money on me. Damn. OK, credit card it is then.

"Here." I check the dashboard clock. There really isn't much time.

Soon after, he hands me the receipt, as well as the

funny sash type thing I'm supposed to hang up on my rear view mirror. I put my car in first and crawl ahead. That's when I notice an innocuous black sedan parked up ahead in the security check area. That's Liam's car, isn't it? The license plate number is the same, I only notice because it ends on '1234'.

I'm just about to drive up next to it to find Liam, when I see a blond-haired man dressed all in black, waving to one of the policemen standing by the barriers blocking our way. That's not Liam! He turns to walk back towards the car, and I recognise him immediately.

He looks just like the detective who killed himself at the airport, just with slightly longer hair. Either it's his ghost, or his doppelganger. Either way, I'm certain he's Nexus. What's he doing with Liam's car, though?

Then the pieces fall into place. Any doubts I may have had before are wiped away. This is how they're going to pin it on Liam: they've planted the bomb in his car, creepy blond man will drive the car onto the train, pretending to be him.

Seeing as Liam isn't here yet and boarding is starting within the next five minutes, there's no way he'll get here in time to stop the attack. Instead, he'll arrive just to take the blame. I can't let that happen!

The scary blond man gets into Liam's sedan and switches it on. Behind me, someone blows their horn loud enough to make me jump. *Shit, I'm blocking the way and attracting attention to myself.* At this rate, I'll definitely be spotted and ruin my element of surprise.

I pull away and straight into the other security check lane, as far away from Liam's car as I can manage. It turns out that the Nexus guy wouldn't have noticed me anyway, because the policeman he had just exchanged words with waves him through the barrier without even checking his car.

Meanwhile, I'm greeted by another copper who knocks on my window.

"Open your boot, please? Routine inspection."

Oh Jesus, you've got to be joking! I force a smile and hit the lever next to my foot. The policeman walks around my vehicle, inspecting it from underneath using one of those mirrors on a stick, before looking inside the back for a moment. I breathe a sigh of relief when he closes the lid shortly after. Hopefully I'll be able to catch up with the guy in Liam's car and see what he's up to now.

"Passport, please," he says when he makes it back to my window.

A cold sweat erupts all over my body. Passport. *Fuck.* I hadn't thought of this.

With shaking fingers, I grab my handbag from the passenger seat and pretend to look for it in there. *Think! What do I do now?* They're not going to let me through without it, and meanwhile the Nexus guy is going to blow up the train and I can't do anything about it!

After wasting a few seconds with my handbag, I open the glove box and rummage around in the papers in there, while shooting the cop an apologetic smile. At least I hope it looks apologetic and not guilty as sin.

"Brixton, help me out for a second, mate," someone shouts.

I look up to find another cop waving at the one waiting for my passport. He excuses himself and steps towards the other barrier, giving me the chance I needed. I wait until he's far enough away, and put my car in first, slam my foot down and race ahead.

"Oi!" the cop shouts, while turning back in my direction. He sprints ahead just as I pull away.

My engine screams, tyres squeal as I try to avoid as much of the barrier as I can by aiming for the little gap towards the right. Metal from my car and the barrier come together in a horrible crash, but my car wins, sort of, and I make it through.

In the rear view mirrors I can see the cops collecting together, shouting into their walkie-talkies as two of them get into a car parked beside the security check area to follow me. My heart is hammering in my throat and my hands still shaking, but I don't slow down even through the winding road heading for the waiting area.

The boards are already instructing people with my

ticket to proceed to check-in, so that's what I do. I ignore the slow speed limit, and speed past slower cars exiting the parking lot. I can't see the black sedan anywhere, but I have to assume he's already nearing the check-in himself.

Behind me I hear sirens, but I dare not look back. I skid through the little roundabout, narrowly avoiding a row of traffic cones as I race ahead, following the signs towards the tunnel. Then the road opens up into at least six lanes.

I ignore the man in the high-visibility vest who is trying to guide me into a queue of waiting cars, instead I overtake all of them and head straight for the large ramp that curves around towards the train station. One queue of cars is already moving so I follow them towards what I assume must be our platform.

Frightened drivers screech to a halt all around while I zig-zag around them. Car horns go off left and right, but I don't let them put me off.

I'm going to be in so much trouble for this! Hopefully they'll believe me when I tell them about the Nexus attack.

Finally, I can see the station, where car after car are already boarding the train. Just as I make it there, narrowly avoiding other vehicles waiting to get on, I see a black car vanish inside the loading area up ahead. There he is! The bastard.

The cops are on my tail, and closing the distance between us fast. Their sirens are getting louder and louder.

I grip the steering tighter, determined not to fail at the last hurdle. Someone needs to stop this train, by any means necessary, or all those people are going to die. I don't see any sign of Liam, and that asshole driving Liam's car has already gotten on unchecked.

There is no other choice, nobody to act but me. I guess this is what they call 'the point of no return'. The pressure to act is immense, I can't and won't fight it.

Checking the rear view mirror one final time, I see the flashing blue lights of the police car right behind me. I put my right foot flat down and jump ahead towards the train, aim for the ramp, sort of. *Fuck it.* I close my eyes and freeze as the car lifts off slightly on the way in, then hits straight into the back wall of the train. A sharp pain shoots through my forehead and all the world goes black.

CHAPTER FIVE   LIAM

I had done my best to reach the tunnel on time, but the roadworks had slowed my progress significantly. By the time I arrived, there was some commotion going on at the entrance. Police were scrambling to chase someone who had broken through the barrier.

I drove inside unchecked with my siren still on and proceeded straight through towards the train terminal. Then, an ambulance raced past me and I couldn't shake the feeling that whatever was going on had something to do with Tess. Ever since her message, I hadn't been able to reach her. She should have stayed away, but I didn't get the chance to convince her. I doubt I would have been able to anyway.

A sick feeling made its way into the pit of my stomach, something horrible has happened to Tess and it's all my fault. I put my foot down and chased the ambulance down.

We turned into the first platform, and there it was: the tail end of her old Nissan was sticking out through the open doors of the train. *Shit.* The cops had cordoned off the area with warning tape already, and the ambulance screeched to a halt just ahead of me.

Of course I'd expected the worst, so seeing the

two paramedics carry her out of the train on an uncovered stretcher rather than in a body bag was somewhat of a relief. I flashed my ID and insisted they let me into the back of the van with her while they administered first aid.

So that's where I am now, watching over her while she's passed out. Her golden hair is fanned out over the stretcher, giving the effect of a halo almost. She looks peaceful, except for the purple bruise on her forehead and cut on her bottom lip.

It hurts to see her like this, and I can't do anything to help her.

"How is she?" I ask the lanky brown-haired paramedic, who doesn't look a day over twenty-one.

"Her vitals are good, pupils are responsive. Just got bumped on the head, is all. We'll know more when she wakes up."

I nod at him and exit the back of the van. As much as I want to just sit there with her, I have a mission to complete here. Obviously she was trying to prevent the attack just as I was meant to, and in a moment of desperation decided that she couldn't stop the train any other way than to plough right into it.

If she wasn't lying on a stretcher in the back of that ambulance right now, the situation would be almost funny.

I scan the surrounding areas for anything suspicious. For anyone or anything that looks out of place.

Up ahead by the perimeter set up by the local police, a group of bystanders has collected. Tourists and businesspeople who were hoping to reach France within the next half hour. Obviously they're not going anywhere for a while now, not until their vehicles can be unloaded and booked onto another train.

Except, one of them *is* going somewhere. A guy in black with short-ish light-blond hair is briskly walking away from the commotion. I speed up to a jog, getting closer to him as he continues to walk without even looking back once. I'm forced to slow down when I try to cross the crowd of onlookers, at which point he does finally turn around.

Our eyes meet, he notices me just as I recognise his face. He's almost a perfect match for the dead Nexus guy lying in the morgue back at HQ. His twin? He sprints away and jumps down onto the track ahead of the train. I follow him at full pelt.

With every step I think of Tess lying in that ambulance. She must have seen him and recognised him as well and done her best to stop whatever he was up to. Now it's up to me to finish the job. I run as fast as my feet will carry me, spurred on by the thought that I owe it to her to catch this motherfucker.

He's not an easy target. Clearly well trained, extremely fit and quick on his feet, he jumps up onto the next platform and resumes running at full speed. I summon all I've got left in me and make it up onto the platform just behind him, channelling all my energy into my legs. The gap between us closes, I can almost hear him pant ahead of me.

The man tries to change direction to evade me, but I jump ahead with my arms stretched out and tackle him onto the hard concrete ground. The impact hurts, despite landing mostly on him. We roll over each other a few times, partially as an effort to disorient him, as well as to avoid serious injury to my knees and shoulders hitting the ground.

"Gotcha!" I shout, while grabbing his throat and keeping him pinned on his back below me.

"You didn't get shit," he spits.

I loosen my fingers around his neck, while wrestling both his arms together, keeping them pinned to the ground underneath my hand which has my whole body weight resting right on top. I find my handcuffs on my belt and restrain him before he gets the chance to wriggle free.

"You wanna tell me where the bomb is or do I have to find out for myself?" I ask. He won't tell, I already know that. But at least I already know it's probably in my car, somewhere inside that train.

He just grins at me, his smug face suggesting he's

either too stupid to realise that he's lost and I've won, or he's just plain crazy. Considering he's Nexus, I'm going to assume he's bat shit insane.

Ignoring the sharp sting in my right knee, I get up, dragging him onto his feet beside me. We both limp back to the first platform, where I can already see one more black sedan, just like my own, parked up beside the police cars. Backup from HQ. As I get closer, I spot Clark pacing around Tess's wrecked car. Bloody great.

I continue to drag the suspect along with me. Whatever happens, I'm sure as hell not handing him over to Clark, the Nexus mole.

"Everson." Clark squints at me suspiciously.

I return an equally distrustful glare. "Clark."

"What's happened here?" He looks at the suspect in my custody, then back at me.

"Nexus trying to blow shit up, same old."

"Uhuh," Clark grunts. "Funny, how Nexus seems to have a real hard-on for involving you and your girlfriend in their little plans, don't you think?"

"Funny, indeed." I stare at him as he stares at me. Neither of us shows signs of backing down.

Tess... I've got to check on Tess. I tear myself away from my little pissing contest with Clark and wrestle the suspect into my car, locking him inside.

"Nobody takes him anywhere without me, you understand?" I bark at Clark, who just shrugs in response. "I'm going to go question Tess if she's awake, but meanwhile, there's still a bomb on board this train, most likely planted in my regular vehicle. I suggest you guys get on that as soon as possible."

At the mention of the word 'bomb', Clark finally stops glaring at me and nods in agreement. He gets his phone out and tells Jenkins to call in the bomb squad, in case we find something that we cannot disarm ourselves. Then he gets the position of my car from Eurotunnel security.

Within moments, they start to evacuate the platform. My stand-in car and the ambulance are the last vehicles to be moved.

I call over the other agent who had arrived in Clark's car and hand him my keys, asking if he can keep an eye on the suspect while I'm inside the ambulance. It's a risk, letting the cuffed man out of my sights, but I simply must see how Tess is doing.

When I open the rear doors of the ambulance and step inside, Tess is still lying there in the same position as when I had checked on her before.

"Updates?" I ask the paramedic, who just shrugs.

"No change."

I sit down and take her hand.

The ambulance jerks into motion, taking us further away from the train and towards safety. Within minutes, we're parked up at the new perimeter and the engine is switched off again.

She looks so fragile. Her hand feels small in mine. What if she won't wake up? What if the paramedic has missed something and she's in a much more serious state than he suspects?

It takes a lot for me not to panic, not to insist they check her again. It's not rational, I shouldn't be dictating how this guy does his job. The truth is, it's not his fault I'm scared for her. It's not even *her* fault, but my own. I involved her in all of this, and now she's gotten hurt. Because of me.

Earlier today, I had been determined to call it quits. For her safety as well as my own self-preservation, I would let her go. I hadn't planned on seeing her again, knowing that the moment I'd lay eyes on her, I'd feel compelled to change my mind.

How could I deny myself the feeling she instilled in me whenever we were together? The sense of belonging, the irresistible urge to try and make her smile, knowing it will light up even the darkest part of me. If she does wake up, she'll be angry with me and I'll deserve it. But won't she understand that *this, right here,* is exactly what I had wanted to prevent? Hopefully she will.

She stirs and my heart skips a whole lot of beats.

"Shhh…" I try to calm her as she struggles to open her eyes with a wild, panicked look on her face. "Don't speak."

CHAPTER SIX

When I wake up, my entire body feels stiff. *Where am I?*

I try to open my eyes and look around, but have to blink against the bright lights surrounding me. I can't see anything clearly, just blurs of colours and blinding white. When I try to speak, my voice doesn't sound like my own, I can only manage a pathetic croak.

"Don't speak," a familiar voice says.

Someone touches my hand, fingers thread through mine. *Ouch, my head.*

I try to reach up to see where the sharp pain is coming from, but can't lift my arm.

"I can't…" I try to say, but the rest of the sentence doesn't make it past my lips.

"You need to rest. You've been in an accident."

I blink again a few times, until finally my eyes adjust to my surroundings. Above me, a concerned pair of eyes meets my own. Beautiful, familiar, green. Dark brown hair frames that face I haven't been able to stop thinking about since last week, against a backdrop of clinical equipment and tubes and things. A hospital? No, there's a lot of commotion nearby, as well as the occasional siren. I must be in an ambulance, still at the Eurotunnel complex.

"Liam," I sigh.

Am I hallucinating? Is he really here? I blink at him in disbelief, half expecting that he'll just vanish on me.

"Yes," he answers.

"Did you get the guy? Did you secure the bomb?" I ask.

He looks away, avoiding my question. Then his eyes are fixed on mine again.

"What were you thinking? Driving your car into a train, really?" He sounds upset. Why is he upset? Did something go wrong?

I don't know how to respond.

"I… Someone had to stop the train," I explain at last.

"I was on my way, I had it under control," he says. "Plus, you could have called in a bomb threat, just like we had agreed at the airport last week."

I press my lips together tightly. The pain in my forehead is getting progressively worse and for the umpteenth time today my eyes start to burn. Ugh. Why is he being such a douche about this? He wasn't here and the car was already on the train. Doesn't he see that something needed to be done right then and there?

"Whatever. I didn't exactly have a lot of time to figure it out." I close my eyes and turn my head away, not wanting him to see my tears. Rather than show the slightest amount of appreciation for what I've done, he seems more intent on giving me a lecture. "What do you care, after today we're probably never seeing each other again!" I complain.

"Agent Everson, are you in here?" That same horrible voice interrupts us, which had done so less than twenty-four hours ago in my own bedroom. The redhead he works for. Ugh, I hate that woman. I refuse to even look in her direction.

"Ma'am," Liam responds.

"How on earth did this civilian end up here again? Please step out and explain why you would go against my orders like that?"

Liam lets go of my hand and does as asked, presumably, but I don't open my eyes. The ambulance door creaks partially shut, though muffled voices of his conversation with his boss are still filtering through loud enough for me to hear every word.

I try to ignore them. It's harder coming face to face with Liam now than I'd thought. It hurts too much to know that he's right there in front of me but I can't have him anymore.

"It's a long story," Liam sighs.

"Did you secure the bomb?" the redhead asks.

"Clark and the local police are on it." Liam sounds impatient.

"And the girl, have you questioned her yet? This time I'd like to debrief her myself as well." *Ugh. I'm not looking forward to that at all.*

"She was knocked out when she drove her car into the train. She's awake now, but it would be best to give her some rest," Liam tries to dissuade his boss. I doubt it will change her mind, but I'm glad he's trying anyway.

"Fine. Nothing promotes clarity like a little rest." My eyes snap wide open at Liam's boss's statement.

A weird saying, one I've heard only once before… Fletch said that to me while he was questioning me in the warehouse yesterday!

Holy shit, does that mean what I think it does? I've got to get off this stretcher, out of this ambulance if that woman is going to come in here and 'debrief' me, whatever that means. In my panic, I knock over a tray with some cotton wool and antiseptic that was probably meant to be used on me at some point, making a loud clattering noise at it hits the floor.

The door opens, and Liam steps inside, looking even more worried than before. "Everything OK in here?"

I can't breathe, and my eyes are about ready to pop out of my head. "Yeah. Fine."

"Right. Be careful." He turns, like he's about to leave again. I can't let that happen.

"Wait," I say.

He pauses, with the door still ajar. I can't be sure if we're overheard, and I can't take the risk if we are.

"Come here for a moment," I whisper.

He looks out for a moment, as if he's unsure what to do. Then he finally steps inside all the way, shutting the door, allowing me to breathe a sigh of relief.

"What is it, Tess?" His voice sounds strangely raw, but I don't have time to analyse his state of mind right now.

"The woman, that weird saying she quoted just now. Nothing promotes clarity like a little rest." As I start to explain, suddenly my genius observation seems a lot stupider than it did in my head. "Yesterday at the warehouse, the guy in charge said exactly that. He said it was something his mother used to say."

"Right." Liam looks me in the eye, I don't know if he's trying to figure out just how badly I got bumped on the head, or if he actually takes me seriously.

"Think about it. Have you ever heard anyone say that?"

"No."

"Me neither." He's right. I sound like a crazy person right now. Just because someone uses a weird turn of phrase doesn't make them a terrorist.

"I'll be right back," Liam says, patting me on my hand and heading straight for the door.

Outside, I don't hear voices anymore, just distant sirens. I try to tell myself I've done my part, and it's up to fate, or Liam, to make sure things work out, but the knot in my chest refuses to budge.

—————•—————

LIAM

Tess's observation seems outlandish, insane, and yet… it would make sense, wouldn't it? What if all this time, the mole inside our unit wasn't an agent, but the team leader? It's perfect, elegant even.

I decide to take a risk, to test the theory. What are the chances of Nexus having multiple people inside our little unit? Low, I'd say. I've already shared my suspicions about Clark with Mrs. H., and what happened? Nothing. She didn't act on it, instead sending Clark out as my backup immediately after. Perhaps because she knew I'm wrong, because she herself is involved.

"Hey, Clark." I catch up with him as he pulls into the wide parking lot. He lowers his window and gives me a nasty stare.

"Everson."

"Threat contained?" I ask.

He nods.

"I'll just come right out and say it. I told H you might be involved with Nexus," I say, while keeping my gaze fixed on him, gauging his reaction.

His eyes widen in surprise.

"But… wait, you did what?!" he exclaims. He's pissed, and rightly so.

Strangely, he doesn't seem concerned though, just angry. He shows no signs of guilt or nervousness.

"When I got the phone call and all of a sudden our prisoner ends up dead, before he tells us anything of use; that didn't look good, you have to admit." I wait as Clark gets out of the car in a huff, slamming the door behind him and getting up close to me with balled fists. What is he going to do, punch me in the face? Let him try.

"Well, similarly you have to admit it didn't look good to accept a phone call from Fletch in the middle of an interrogation, to lie about it, and then to run off, leaving me to deal with a dead witness. How do I know you're not the one who's involved?"

"Touché," I say.

We're only a few inches apart now. His forehead is turning sweaty, his cheeks are flushed with residual anger, and he seems to be completely tense. Every muscle in his body seems to be preparing for a fight. So that's his story. While I'm suspecting him of wrongdoing, he's doing the same to me. It makes sense.

"Don't you think it's strange that after I told her about my suspicions, nothing happened? Similarly, she didn't hold me, just put me back on active duty, presumably against your advice."

"That's right. I insisted she keep you locked up at least until we could figure out what was happening here with your vehicle."

He continues to stare me down, but I don't break eye contact.

"Perhaps the reason she ignored us both was that she already knew we were wrong," I say.

"How do you mean?" Clark looks surprised again, though the twitching in his jaw muscle betrays that he's still seething under the surface.

"Perhaps she's the mole." As I say the words out loud, I see something click in Clark's eyes. As if a little switch is flicked and all sorts of puzzle pieces that previously didn't have a place, fall into place in his mind.

He takes a deep breath and thinks for a moment. His body language changes: his muscles seem to relax as he considers my words, comparing them to his own observations and suspicions. The Clark I've known for the past seven years is back.

I tell him about Tess's observation, assuring him that I trust her. There is no way my meeting with her was anything other than a coincidence. She's an innocent in all of this, and has had the misfortune to spend over an hour in Fletch's presence, before I intervened.

"I can't believe I'm saying this, but…" Clark sighs again, scratching the back of his head. "That actually makes a lot of sense. Now what?"

Before I get the chance to respond, his walkie-talkie crackles and H's voice breaks through the static, asking for his position.

"Outside the perimeter, Ma'am," Clark replies, while keeping his gaze fixed on me.

"Change of mission. We have reason to believe that Everson was involved in the attack after all. His intervention was just a clever ruse. You must stop him, by any means necessary," Mrs. H orders.

"Understood. By any means?"

"I authorise you to use lethal force."

That's it, irrefutable proof of what I've just told him.

Clark instinctively puts his hand on his holster as he places the walkie-talkie back onto his belt.

"I'm going to have to take you in, old mate," he says.

I'm about to protest, to argue in favour of everything I've just told him, but he doesn't give me the chance to speak.

"You heard the lady. Let's not make things difficult, all right?" Clark says as he approaches me with handcuffs at the ready.

CHAPTER SEVEN

Shortly after Liam leaves, I'm getting checked out by a paramedic. Apparently I'm all good, no sign of injuries other than the obvious bump on my forehead and sore bottom lip. Not even a concussion. They decide I don't need to be taken to hospital, and I'm grateful for their assessment.

Even if I'd been in a critical condition, they couldn't have dragged me away from what might as well be the last time I get to see Liam. Only, he hasn't returned yet.

I wait around the ambulance for ages, wondering whether to make myself scarce before the scary redhead comes back to *debrief* me or whatever it is she wanted. If I am right, and the painful cramp in my gut still seems convinced that I am, sticking around isn't just potentially annoying, it could also be dangerous. What if she suspects that I know? My safety could be at stake. Again.

Right now I could really use Liam's advice. Do I stay? Do I run? If I run, they'll just find me again. The woman knows where I live, for God's sake. I don't even know if he managed to catch the guy who was driving his car earlier. I don't know a damn thing, and it's driving me crazy.

"Are you all right?" the paramedic asks.

I realise I'm still sitting on the back steps of the van, despite him telling me that I could go.

"Uh, yeah. Sorry. It's just, I don't have a car or anything," I mumble, while getting up.

He smiles at me weirdly. His expression is almost sarcastic, *you would still have a car if you hadn't driven it into a train earlier.* So helpful.

There's nowhere else to go, nothing else to do, so I sit down on the kerb next to the ambulance instead. I may not be seriously hurt, but my head is still pretty sore and I'm exhausted.

The policemen who were chasing me earlier are parked nearby and eyeing me suspiciously. I'm surprised they haven't arrested me. Perhaps Liam, or someone from his unit explained the situation.

"Miss Aldershot." Liam's boss, the scary redhead approaches from behind the ambulance. "There you are. If you don't mind, I'd like to ask you a few questions."

I swallow hard, and rub my palms on my trousers, trying to get rid of the instant cold sweat that's appeared.

"Sure. No problem."

"Please join me inside the tactical van?" She points to a black van parked nearer to the ramp leading towards the train station. "We'll have some privacy in there."

I nod, but don't say anything. If I refuse, it'll create suspicion. At the same time, I really don't want to be alone in the back of a van with a potential terrorist either. It's a lose-lose situation.

Reluctantly, I follow her inside, where she gestures over to the bench along the side wall of the van. I take a seat and wait while she closes the doors. It's so small in here, so stuffy. My heart is racing and my vision goes slightly blurry. I wonder if that's just because of the accident.

"Are you all right, you look pale?" the woman asks, while taking a seat opposite me.

I nod and stare at the floor.

"Fine. Just tired."

"All right. How about you start by telling me how you knew to come here today?" Her blue eyes bore into me.

It makes me uneasy, the way she continues to stare at me like a human lie detector. I'm certain she'll be able to tell if I hide anything from her.

"I overheard a phone conversation by some guy who works at the airport. He was talking about agents, the tunnel, and Nexus," I say.

"Who?"

"I don't know the guy." A cold sweat is starting to collect on my palms. Although I'm not lying, I don't actually *know* Alec at all, of course I still know more about him than I'm letting on.

She squints slightly, as if focusing on me extra hard is going to uncover what's going in my head. She can tell, can't she? My throat goes dry, forcing me to swallow. God, I wish I was a better liar!

"And how did you end up at the airport last week?" she asks.

Shit, didn't Liam tell her what happened? How he got into my car? If I answer this one wrong, I might get him into trouble again! I don't know how to respond, so I try to buy time by faking a cough.

The redhead impatiently taps her foot as she waits for my response with her arms crossed, when the back door of the van swings open. The first face I see is Liam's, only things don't look quite right. Then I see the other agent, Clark, shoving him inside with his hand on Liam's shoulder. *Shit.*

"What the!" I exclaim in shock.

"Ma'am, here he is." Clark nods at the redhead, and pushes Liam further forward, before shutting the van door behind him.

"This is bullshit," Liam says. He avoids eye contact with me as he passes me by. His hands are cuffed behind his back.

"Shut up!" Clark responds, while elbowing him in the shoulder.

I don't know what to say or how to react anymore. After all that, Liam coming in after me and trying to prevent the attack from happening, he's back in cuffs?

What the hell do these people want?

"Brilliant timing. Your girlfriend was about to elaborate on her involvement with Nexus. You might as well do the same." The redhead triumphantly looks around the room, at me, then Clark, who seems extremely proud of himself, and Liam, who looks a lot less like a classy government agent and a lot more angry bad boy right now.

I can't deal with this. All the strains of the day wash over me again, filling my eyes with tears. I'm sick of crying. I'm so sick of shit going wrong as well. Fuck.

I hide my face in my hands and wish I could just disappear.

"I will do no such thing," Liam argues.

"Oh, sooner or later, they all talk," Clark butts in.

"Very clever, to arrange for your car to be stolen from HQ to try and demonstrate your innocence. It's lucky Clark noticed the secondary circuit to disarm the bomb, or we might have still had a huge mess on our hands even after the train was stopped," the redhead says. Most of her words might as well be Greek, that's as much sense as they make.

"That's right, the secondary circuit. Very well hidden it was too," Clark's voice sounds subtly different. Less macho and celebratory, more thoughtful.

I look up to find him staring ahead, his full focus

shifted from Liam to her. Odd.

"Good job," she responds, seemingly oblivious to his change in demeanour.

"Interestingly, it was Liam who pointed out that the bomb would still be on the train, after apprehending a Nexus guy on the platform," Clark says.

"He's good at covering his tracks, but not *that* good."

I look at Liam, who is also staring at the redhead. There's something different about him, he's tense, but his anger doesn't seem to be directed at Clark, who brought him in here in cuffs, but at *her,* their boss.

"Now," Liam whispers, Clark jumps into action, draws his gun and points it at the redhead.

I let out a surprised scream, then cover my mouth with both hands when I see Liam's wrists have somehow freed themselves of his restraints. He lurches forward, going straight for her arm, which is instinctively reaching out for her own weapon. The struggle is over in a fraction of a second, leaving me breathless as my brain tries to comprehend what has just happened.

"I'll have your jobs," the redhead spits, while Liam puts her in cuffs this time.

"Yeah, right," Clark remarks. He rests his hands on his hips, straightening his broad shoulders. "I wasn't quite sure whether to believe Liam when he came to me earlier, but you've managed to clear things up wonderfully with your little *secondary circuit* remark. You couldn't have known about that, because I hadn't told anyone, not even Jenkins."

The redhead glares at Clark, pressing her lips together tightly into a straight line.

Liam drags her toward Clark, handing her over to him, then comes up to me.

"Are you all right?" he asks. His voice soothes me, almost making me forget how scared I was only seconds ago.

I nod. "Fine."

"I know you think this makes a difference, but it doesn't!" the redhead shouts from behind Liam, prompting him to turn around.

"Oh? The attack has been stopped, the mole in our unit found and arrested, seems like a win to me," Liam remarks.

"Someone will take over. Fletch cannot die," she says with a sinister smile forming on her lips.

"Certainly looked like he did last night," Liam replies.

"Oh, him! He was just a meaningless pawn. Nexus is bigger than any of you can imagine!"

I raise my eyebrows, watching her. Everything about her has changed. She had seemed so strict and controlled every time I'd seen her, and now, the complete opposite. She must be losing it.

"Right…" Liam turns his back to her and gestures at me to get up. I lose myself in his arms, where finally, after the most tumultuous day ever, I start to feel safe.

"Mark my words! Nexus will prevail!"

Her tirade is interrupted by Clark's phone, which he answers with a comically calm 'hello'.

"Really? Interesting. Thanks, Jenkins." Clark hangs up and grins widely at Liam and me.

"Guess what, they've identified the body from the warehouse. He shares a surprising amount of DNA with someone we know." He gestures over at the redhead beside him by nodding his head.

"That's very interesting indeed." Liam wraps his arms around me tighter, making my heart beat a whole lot faster.

"Before they take you away, just answer me this: why?" Clark asks.

She presses her lips together tightly, but then gives in to the temptation to speak anyway. "Why does everything has to have a reason? Maybe I did it all because it feels good to be bad?" she taunts him.

"I'm not buying it. Are you buying it?" Liam asks Clark, who responds by shaking his head. "Never mind. Once they search her home, and pull apart every last detail of her life and family background, something is bound to make sense," Liam remarks.

"You'll regret this," the redhead snarls. Her face is

a deep crimson as well now, her features tightened by rage. Within less than a second, she turns around, slipping out from underneath Clark's grasp on her shoulder, and grabs his weapon right from the holster on his hip. Having her wrists cuffed together behind her back doesn't hinder her at all as she aims the gun at us by twisting her hand around through the gap between her arm and side. A loud bang shatters through the air, originating right next to my head.

It deafens me instantly, filling my ears with a persistent, all consuming buzz.

The redhead sinks to the ground, and Liam drags me backwards, away from the bloody mess. I don't know how to react, but cannot force myself to look away.

Although he's here with me, I feel like I'm on my own in the van, alone in my head, with only that dead body and the growing pool of blood on the floor to give me company.

Slowly, muffled voices emerge from the white noise surrounding me.

"Tess… Tess… I'm so sorry, Tess, are you OK?"

It's Liam. I look up at him, and his green eyes are full of concern.

"Yeah. Can we go now?" I ask, before noticing my knees buckle involuntarily.

He catches me before I sink to the ground, and carries me out of the van. I don't try to think about what I've just gone through, but can't help looking back anyway.

"Liam," I whisper.

"Yeah," he says, while walking away from the commotion surrounding the van. Agents and police rushing in and out, taking notes and pictures, a couple of them joining Clark, presumably so he can explain what has just happened.

"Don't leave me now." Although I'm literally being too clingy, I'm too frazzled to care.

He lowers me slightly, allowing me another look into his eyes.

"I won't. I'm so sorry."

CHAPTER EIGHT   LIAM

After the surprising twist, ending in H's death, I vowed that things would change. Of course I would have to give a statement, to explain what exactly went down inside the van, but I knew Clark would cover for me at least for a while.

My first priority was to take Tess away from there, away from all the death. Even though the paramedics had released her, saying she was fine, I insisted she get herself checked by a nearby hospital as well. By the time they saw her at the emergency room and confirmed that she was indeed fine, another hour had passed.

We were too far from home and it was already too late to attempt the drive, so I opted for a nearby hotel instead.

She didn't say much on our drive there, just went through the motions until we reached the room.

That's where we are now. In a quaint hotel room in a village near Folkestone, where neither of us have ever been before, or perhaps will return to in future. She's still quiet, sitting on the bed, staring at the wall, and although I wish I knew what was going on in her head, I'm afraid to ask, opting to pace around the room instead.

"I'm so sorry about everything that happened today," I start, at first wondering whether she's even hearing me, until her eyes meet mine and I recognise that I have her attention.

"We won, right?" Her voice sounds bleak.

"Right."

"So then what's there to be sorry about?"

I think for a moment. A lot, actually. I have a lot to be sorry about. She knows it too, adding to the current awkwardness. The magnetism between us made us gravitate towards each other while in danger, but now that the threat is over, the memories of what came before have flooded back.

"Earlier today, when I said our lives were incompatible..."

Her eyes widen, and I think I see more of a sheen form on them. I've seen fearful looks on so many people over the years, but I can't stand seeing *her* like this.

"I just want you to be safe," I try to explain.

She continues to stare at me without saying a word. It's like being stabbed right in the heart; a type of hurt I've never felt before meeting her. Physical pain I can deal with, it's easy, but this is impossible to tune out.

"This thing between us, I don't understand it. It's all new to me. I know that rationally, we shouldn't get involved. I should leave you to live your life. Safe. Far away from all the shit that my past and my job brings with it."

"You saved my life three times already. Or was it four?" Her tone is still low, though I know she feels as hurt as I do, if not more so. And that makes everything worse. "I feel safe with you."

"It doesn't count if I caused the situation you needed saving from."

"If you say so," she mumbles. She looks away, like she wants to avoid me and the topic of conversation altogether.

I know I should follow through and let her go. It's the right thing to do, but the more I think about it, the more it hurts.

"Anyway, I've said what I had to. I've explained my reasons. But the truth is…" I pause for a moment when her eyes are back on me again. How is it that just a look can throw me off my game completely? How can one person have that much power over me? "I don't think I *can* let you go."

Her eyes widen again, not with fear this time, but hope and recognition.

"No?" she asks.

"No." I shake my head to make my point. There is no way I can turn my back on her now. "I mean… I think I…" I'm not sure I can bring myself to say the words.

My heart is racing now, I - who normally doesn't

know fear - am actually scared about what's going to happen if I complete that thought.

"You what?" she whispers.

To hell with it. She's still here, she seems to like me well enough despite everything.

"I think I love you," I say.

She doesn't respond, at least not verbally. Her gaze seems to soften as she continues to look at me. Her body language demonstrates relief; how her formerly tense posture has relaxed just slightly. I guess I haven't scared her off. Shit, this whole situation is so surreal, I must be losing my mind.

Finally, she does stir. She gets up from the bed and takes a couple of steps to bridge the distance between us. By the time she stretches out her arms and invites me in, I can finally breathe a sigh of relief as well.

"I need to know you're not going to change your mind again. That you're not going to avoid me again, whether you think it's for my own good or not. We've got to be upfront and honest with each other, and actually *talk*." She presses herself against me while she speaks, making it hard for me to think clearly.

"I won't. I promise." I close my eyes and just focus on her presence in my arms.

"You know, before you came along the most exciting thing that had ever happened to me was when my local Chinese takeaway added some Thai food to their menu. Your life has too much excitement, mine too little. I don't think that's necessarily a bad thing."

She releases herself from my embrace slightly, stands on tiptoes and gives me a peck on my lips. Instantly, my body reacts. Worries are wiped away, concerns seem less important. I want her with all my being, keep her safe, make her happy, see her smile.

Most of all, right now, I want to prove to her that I really mean everything I've said. I do love her, I just didn't recognise it earlier.

I pick her up, rejoicing when she wraps her arms around my neck like it's become second nature to her. We've done this before, and it was good. Today it will be better.

She kisses my neck, her breath tickling me slightly, but not unpleasantly so. Her body is so inviting, soft and lush. I can't think of a single thing I would change about this moment, or about her. She is perfection.

When I lay her down on the bed, the way she looks at me confirms it: she loves me too. People say they know when someone is the one for them, and I'd never understood how that was possible. Now I know.

We may come from different worlds, but somehow when we're together, everything makes sense.

She starts unbuttoning her blouse, revealing more

and more tempting ivory skin. I can't resist, diving down for a taste.

Of all the women I've ever been with - and there have been a few - none managed to captivate me like she does. None were as beautiful, as sexy. I feel like I haven't even scratched the surface, like there is so much more I have to discover about her. Although I hadn't wanted to involve her in my world due to the danger it poses, I desperately want to find out everything about hers.

I want to share Chinese takeaway meals, and boring drives in rattly old cars through the evening rush hour on the A4. One day, with her, I can imagine having more than I'd ever planned for myself: perhaps even a clichéd white picket fence around the home we share.

"I know it's too soon, but I love you too," she breathes, as I run my hands over her curves. "From the moment you got into my car and I threatened you with my deodorant, I knew there was something different about you."

"Lush Lavender, as I recall." I let out a chuckle, as does she.

"I was improvising." I cut off her justification with a deep kiss. Her taste is intoxicating, as is her scent. Floral, feminine, fresh despite the long, trying day we've both had.

She reaches for my T-shirt, lifting it up as far as

she can manage, until I take it off all the way. I love the way her hands feel on me. There is never any hesitation, not even when she caresses my back. I appreciate that she hasn't asked how I got those scars, like she understands that some things are best left alone until the time is right.

Underneath me, we each fumble with the remainder of our clothes, eager - desperate - to get rid of them all. Without any more barriers, we come together skin to skin. Although I'm aching to feel our bodies join again, I take my time.

I can't imagine not having this, not having her in my life anymore. Crazy as it may seem, we've known each other less than a week. We've made our choice, to open up to one another. To show weakness in admitting our feelings, hoping that it may give us strength for whatever is to come.

Now, at least for tonight, we have all the time in the world.

I look down at her, how her hair frames her beautiful face. Her eyes beg me for more kisses, more caresses. I cannot resist.

Slipping my hand in between us, I guide myself into her. The moan that passes her lips makes me desperate for more. I start to move, watching the change in her expression as pleasure fills her.

For me, as I imagine is the same for most men, sex had always been a necessity, like air or water. But with her, it's so much more than that. It's the ultimate expression of what I feel for her. Whatever the future may hold, this is the one way I can ensure she's satisfied in this moment.

Her arms wrap around me tightly, as if to keep me buried deep inside her. I gather her up in my arms, lifting her against me, as I continue to thrust into her. Deeper. Faster.

Our bodies are perfectly in tune, as if subconsciously we already know one another. If I shift my weight, angle my hips slightly forward, I know she will moan into my ear. When she nibbles on my earlobe, and kisses my neck, I'm sure she knows I get goosebumps.

That's how we tease each other, heightening the other's pleasure until we reach the point of no return. They say simultaneous orgasms are rare and most couples don't have them. We do. I like to think that's a sign.

She starts first, bucking her hips up at me, involuntarily digging her fingernails into my shoulders. That's my cue to let go, release the tension that's built up throughout our time together. I close my eyes, and focus on her voice as she moans my name.

My mind goes blank. The feeling is indescribable. Fireworks. That's all I can relate this to.

Sweet pleasure surges through me, until it seems to

explode.

The aftershocks last for at least a minute.

I shift my weight off her, but am not in a rush to let her go completely.

Muscles relax again. Our breaths still slowly.

Her hand on my shoulder rests right above the painful reminders of a memory I haven't spoken about in fifteen years.

"I was eleven when my mum remarried," I start.

She doesn't reply, but the slight stir of her finger tells me she's listening.

"And I was fourteen when she was widowed." I close my eyes, resting my forehead against the side of Tess's face. It's not easy to find the words, but it feels important that she knows.

"He had always been mean, but for years they both hid his real nature from me. I didn't come to know until one day I came home early from school and caught him beating her. When I tried to stop him, he turned on me with a belt."

Tess wraps her arms around me tighter, giving me the courage to continue.

"She was in a bad state, but still she tried to drag him away from me. He instantly went at her, punishing her for intervening, I managed to get the belt from him. I think he underestimated how strong I'd become over the years. I looped the belt through the buckle, slipped it over his head and dragged him backwards, allowing her to flee. I don't remember clearly what happened after that, only that I still sat there in that room, the belt taut in my fist, when the police arrived. He was dead on the floor."

It's crazy how something from so long ago can still have an effect today. A cold sweat has developed on my forehead and in my palms. Still, Tess doesn't let go, she continues to hold on to me, soothing me with gentle caresses.

"They decided it was self-defence, but I was institutionalised in a psychiatric facility for a while anyway. Mum couldn't deal with what had happened and took her own life shortly after, so Child Protection put me in a home. That's where the guy who founded our unit recruited me years later. They were looking for people who fit a specific profile: capable of violence, but only for a cause. No family."

The room is silent when I stop talking. All I can hear is her regular breaths, and the persistent drum of my heart filling my ears.

"I'm so sorry that happened to you," Tess whispers finally.

"I'm not," I say. "I don't want pity, I just need you to know who I am."

"I don't pity you, I love you. There's a difference. I understand now."

I look up, and indeed find that expression isn't one of pity. Her eyes seem to shine, a smile breaks through her lips as she beckons me closer. The kiss that follows confirms it: she loves me for all that I am.

EPILOGUE

"Status update," I say, while swallowing the lump that tends to develop in my throat whenever Liam is in the field. I'm scared for his safety, of course I am. But he's capable and Clark has his back.

"We're in pursuit of two suspects, armed and dangerous, heading up the M1 in a stolen black SUV. We've just passed Exit 9," Liam responds. The line crackles slightly, and I can hear Clark remark something about the traffic in the background.

"Understood. Air backup is on the way, I'll soon be able to update you in real time once I have eyes on the road. Be advised that Exit 10, two miles from your position is shut with roadworks, though the suspects may opt to break through the barrier in an attempt to evade you. It's a dead end, so they'll be forced to stop." I zoom into the satellite image of the road ahead, searching for more possible escape routes, but there aren't any.

"No problem. We're ready."

"Good luck."

"Thanks, Tess. We'll get them." Although the conversation is over for now, we keep the line live for future updates.

Within minutes, the helicopter I'd called in catches

up and its video feed pops up on my screen. The SUV swerves through the traffic, with Liam and Clark hot on their heels. Every move the suspects make, they copy. Clark is great behind the wheel, there's no way they'll get away.

As the roadworks come into view, I brace myself for what's about to happen. This is the moment of truth: was I right about the exit? Sure enough, the SUV swerves to the left and races through the coned-off slip road. Clark pulls in just behind him, when the driver of the SUV realises what a mistake he's made and slams on his brakes.

Clark and Liam's black sedan narrowly avoids a collision, as the SUV skids to a halt, and the driver attempts to turn the vehicle around in order to head back onto the motorway. Before he gets the chance to do any of that, Clark has blocked his way with their car and Liam is already out, with his gun drawn.

I forget to breathe while watching it all unfold. Crouching behind the sedan, Liam aims and fires in the SUV's direction. The suspects respond with counter shots. This back and forth continues for another minute or so, until Liam hits one of the SUV's tyres, as well as the windscreen, which shatters.

Obviously the video feed from the chopper has no sound, so I can only imagine Liam shouting at the suspects to surrender themselves if they want to live. Sure enough, two figures exit the SUV with their

ABOUT THE AUTHOR

Dear Reader,

Perhaps you've been following me for a while, perhaps you're new to my work. Still, I'd like to give you a little background.

My writing career started all the way back in October 2012 when I took a very deep breath, closed my eyes, crossed my fingers and even my toes and clicked 'Publish' on my first steamy short story. That story was called Ladies' Day and that, and the novella it spawned eventually (Beautiful Stranger) are surprisingly relevant today because it also features a curvy leading lady.

Since then, I wrote and published a whole bunch of other books, in various romance sub genres; as L. Moone I write contemporary, and as Lorelei Moone I write about shifters, vampires and other paranormals. Certain themes tend to repeat themselves throughout my catalogue.

Beauty lies in the eye of the beholder. The hang-ups

we tend to have about ourselves and our bodies usually aren't shared by the opposite sex. While it's a lot more popular to write about gorgeous curvy ladies and their athletic admirers than the other way around, I've covered both. More often than not, you'll find a larger man paired up with a petite woman in my catalogue as well (Husky Men Do It Better series).

Love at first sight is another theme I write about quite a lot, both in my paranormal books as well as the contemporary ones. In fact, I have an entire series called Chance Encounters that follows three couples who casually hook up, only to find that they don't really want to say goodbye after. What they recognized as lust, turned out to be something a lot more intimate.

If I had to pick a third, then it would be messed up characters. Perfection is boring to me because if you put two flawless people together there's no conflict; no drama! Some of my characters have physical flaws, while others might be a bit neurotic or otherwise eccentric. That's what keeps things interesting for me as a writer.

For this book, my inspiration was slightly different. Together with a friend of mine, we both decided to write a fun (non-paranormal) romantic suspense. It's got the inevitable alpha male secret agent hero with a heart of gold, and the girl-next-door who finds herself involved in all sorts of craziness all of a sudden. After starting off completely out of her element, the heroine finds her place in this strange new world and even gets a chance to make a difference in the end! I was heavily influenced by the movie Knight and Day, which perfectly combines the excitement, romance and humor I was aiming for in this book.

And that's enough from me. I hope you enjoyed the story as much as I did while writing it, and if you're interested in reading more of my work, perhaps you'll consider signing up for my newsletter. I'll even give you a free short story when you sign up.

x Lorelei

FIND ME AT:

- ❖ LMoone.com
- ❖ Lorelei Moone on Facebook
- ❖ AuthorLMoone on Instagram

I also write Paranormal Romance as Lorelei Moone. Check out LoreleiMoone.com for more information.

For a limited time, all new mailing list subscribers will receive a FREE short story, called At First Sight.

Claim your free copy here:

LMoone.com

Look for the newsletter sign-up form at the bottom of the page.

www.ingramcontent.com/pod-product-compliance
Lightning Source LLC
Chambersburg PA
CBHW070958180726
48291CB00004B/1353